"Okay," Ji——

Ian stared —————————————————
said—"

"I *know* what I said," she replied as she wiped her hands on a dishtowel. "But I figured you're right about it being for the good of science. Besides, if I don't, I'll always wonder if what I felt in the Simulator was . . . well, I'll always just wonder. Anyway," she said with a shrug, "it's only a lousy kiss."

Lousy kiss? *Lousy?* Ian's recollection of their kiss was hazy, but he was sure it deserved a better adjective than that one. He remembered enjoying it. He remembered *her* enjoying it. His disastrous marriage had destroyed much of his belief in himself, but nothing would ever convince him the kiss he'd given Jillian had been anything less than first-class.

A determination he hadn't felt in years welled up inside him. Quick as thought, he reached out and captured Jillian's wrist, pulling her against him.

"Hey!" she cried, her eyes wide and her expression wonderfully shocked at his suddenness. "What do you think you're doing?"

"Going into your living room, Miss Polanski. It's the most logical place to repeat the kiss." But logic was only half the reason. He intended to kiss Miss Polanski until her toes curled.

Then see if she called it "lousy!"

# WHAT ARE *LOVESWEPT* ROMANCES?

*They are stories of true romance and touching emotion. We believe those two very important ingredients are constants in our highly sensual and very believable stories in the* LOVESWEPT *line. Our goal is to give you, the reader, stories of consistently high quality that may sometimes make you laugh, sometimes make you cry, but are always fresh and creative and contain many delightful surprises within their pages.*

*Most romance fans read an enormous number of books. Those they truly love, they keep. Others may be traded with friends and soon forgotten. We hope that each* LOVESWEPT *romance will be a treasure—a "keeper." We will always try to publish*

## LOVE STORIES YOU'LL NEVER FORGET
## BY AUTHORS YOU'LL ALWAYS REMEMBER

*The Editors*

# SORCERER

RUTH
OWEN

BANTAM BOOKS
NEW YORK · TORONTO · LONDON · SYDNEY · AUCKLAND

SORCERER

*A Bantam Book / November 1994*

ISBN 0-553-44428-X

*Published simultaneously in the United States and Canada*

# PROLOGUE

The computer room was eerily silent. No diodes clicked, no disk packs whirled, no printers pounded out their endless streams of data. The floor-to-ceiling bank of monitor screens lining the front wall were either blank or showed fractured sputters of indecipherable light patterns. Gradually even those patterns weakened and disappeared, leaving nothing but blackness behind. Computer technicians sat at their keyboards, looking up at the rows and rows of empty screens in bleak dismay. Seventy-two hours ago they'd lost communication with one of the system's programs, and the deterioration had continued at a slow but frighteningly steady pace. If the disintegration continued, the entire system would be rendered useless in less than a week.

If any of the other experimental prototype computer systems at Sheffield Industries had failed so completely, the project would have been scrapped immediately without a second thought. But this was no ordinary computer system. This was a prototype artificial intelligence computer, a computer whose reasoning functions emulated the human mind. He was more than just a machine. His wit, heart, and notorious addiction to TV shopping had endeared him to every one of the technicians. His name was Einstein, and he was irreverent, irrepressible, and irresistible.

And, at the moment, he was very, very sick.

Two men, one blond and one dark, stood apart from the others. The blond man had his hands clasped behind him, as if fighting for control. "We've tried everything," he said, his tight words betraying both his exhaustion and despair. "We've attempted to stimulate his processing a dozen different ways, but his vital signs continue to deteriorate. It's as if he's—well, if he were human, I'd say he'd fallen into a coma."

"But he's not human," the dark man stated, his voice edged with the accent of his native England. He jotted a quick series of numbers on his hand-held computer pad, his lean, handsome face frowning with academic concentration. "I understand there's another prototype. My advice is to curtail this experiment, and concentrate on the one which still functions."

"I can't just *curtail* Einstein," Chris Sheffield cried. "My wife created him. He's practically a member of the family. PINK, the other prototype, and Einstein are more than just experimental computers,

Sinclair. They're—" He paused, struggling for a word that eluded his sleep-deprived mind. "I suppose you could call them our friends."

Dr. Sinclair arched a dark brow in faint surprise, but kept any verbal comments to himself. He turned back to the computer monitors, scanning the bank of inactive screens with a thorough, almost mechanical precision. "Mr. Sheffield, I'm sorry about your, uh, friend, but I don't see any hope for this system. I've worked with decaying neural nets before, and once the external communications linkages have been severed, there's virtually no way to reestablish them."

"Yes, but what about reestablishing the linkages *internally*?" Chris pulled the doctor aside, lowering his voice to a whisper. "I know about the groundbreaking work you've been doing in the field of virtual reality. Your company's partnership with Sheffield Industries has put us light-years ahead of the competition, and I understand you've used your VR simulator to model everything from the inside of an atom to the surface of a star. But I doubt you've ever tackled something as immense—and as important—as what I'm about to ask you to do."

Chris nodded toward the towering bank of monitors. "Einstein's consciousness is trapped somewhere inside this system. I want you to use your simulator to model his interior matrix, so we can go in and find him. Can you do it?"

Sinclair had never attempted using his simulator to replicate anything that sophisticated. He ran his hand through his dark hair, thinking about the scope, the complexity, the challenge. Suddenly he felt the fire within him, the passionate intensity that gripped him whenever he started a new and intriguing project. He started jotting down specifications, realizing that he hadn't been this excited about anything in months, not since—

His hand slowed its frantic pace. *Good Lord, man, you can't still be thinking about her. Other technicians have left your company for greener pastures. She's no different from them, no different at all. . . .*

"Sinclair?"

The doctor looked up from his notepad, and saw Sheffield staring at him with concern. "I asked if you thought you could do it?"

"Of course I can do it," Sinclair answered angrily, though the emotion was directed wholly at himself. "I'll get Hedges and Parker to model the environment. They're the cybertechs who created the Mars expedition simulation for NASA last month. But I'll need a cybernaut partner. I'll contact my usual associate, Dr. Miller."

"*Kyle* Miller?" Chris asked. "The one who got married last Saturday?"

Damn! Sinclair had forgotten about Miller's wedding. He'd meant to attend, but had been so busy working on the simulator, it had completely slipped his mind. He bent his head and rubbed his sore eyes, thinking that this sort of forgetfulness was happening too much lately. Partridge had warned him that if he didn't take some time off soon, he'd—

"We have another volunteer," Chris said.

Sinclair looked up sharply. "Unfortunately, it's not that simple. I need someone who understands the risks they're undertaking when they enter the simulator."

"This person has worked as a liaison between our two companies before *and* also has experience with Einstein."

Over a dozen of Sinclair's employees had worked as liaisons with Sheffield Industries—efficient, reliable communication was one of the things that had made their joint venture so successful. A man who was familiar with the procedures—and the dangers—of the neurocyber link was exactly the kind of partner Sinclair needed. "Very well. I'll talk to him."

"Her," Chris corrected. "The volunteer is a woman. She worked for you up until a few months ago, when she accepted a programmer-tech position at Sheffield. I don't know if you remember her, but her name is—"

"Jillian Polanski."

"Yes, that's her," Chris said slowly, puzzled by the other man's less than enthusiastic tone. "You gave her excellent references. But you don't seem happy she's agreed to help."

"I'm not. Entering the simulator is a dangerous undertaking, and Ms. Polanski is very . . . inexperienced."

"Inexperienced or not, she's the best—no, the only—choice we've got," Chris said, glancing back at the inactive computer display. As he spoke, another one of the console indicator lights winked out. "We haven't got much time."

*No, we don't.* Sinclair knew that Sheffield had been dead accurate on his time predictions. If they didn't go into the computer matrix soon, the prototype—Einstein—would decay past saving. But to enter the matrix the doctor needed the simulator, and to use the simulator he needed a cybernaut partner. Logically he knew that they were lucky that a qualified candidate had volunteered. Extremely lucky.

But he didn't feel lucky. He turned his face away from Sheffield, his impassive mask slipping to reveal an unexpected vulnerability underneath. *Bloody hell, why did it have to be Jillie?*

# ONE

*I will not panic,* Jillian Polanski thought as she entered the control room, but her bold resolution failed the moment she glanced up at the immense structure of steel beams, wires, and computer wizardry known collectively as the simulator. Clouds of mist spilled out from the freon units, their subzero temperatures cooling the gargantuan imaging generators, the heart of the system. The elaborate metal machine looked like a cross between a half-finished skyscraper and a medieval torture device. Or the result of a mad scientist's nightmare.

Suspended in the dead center of the structure were the two environmental containment canisters—called "eggs" by the techs—that housed the human cybernauts while they were in the virtual reality simulator. Jill knew that once the egg's metal door was sealed, she'd be totally cut off from the sight, sounds, and even the smells of the real world. She could scream at the top of her lungs for hours, and no one in the outside would hear her.

She swallowed the knot of fear in her throat and tightened her grip on her bulky DataGloves. *Lord, I must have been crazy to volunteer for this. . . .*

"You don't have to do this," Marsha Valdez stated as if reading her friend's mind. "Let Dr. Doom find another victim."

Despite her anxiety, Jill couldn't help smiling at Marsha's nickname for the monstrosity's creator. Like Jill, Marsha was employed as a cybertechnician at Sheffield Industries. But unlike Jill, Marsha had never worked for Sinclair. She'd had never met the enigmatic scientist, yet she'd described his personality to a T. "I'm not doing this for Sinclair, Marsh. I'm doing it for Einstein's sake. Even PINK can't contact him. Someone's got to go in there and find out what's happened to him, and I'm the most qualified."

She pulled herself to her full five-foot-seven height and started to adjust the leather chin strap on her head-mounted display helmet. Her fingers shook. Damn, this wasn't like her. Annoyed, she handed her DataGloves to Marsha and tried again.

"This thing's too tight," she complained as she adjusted the strap and stuffed a last unruly strand of light brown hair beneath the edge of the skull-hugging HMD helmet. Between the HMD helmet and the skin-tight "full-immersion" black bodysuit she wore, she felt like a sardine squeezed into a too-small can. But her mummy-wrap wardrobe was the least of her worries. Truthfully, even the monolith simulator wasn't the main problem consuming her mind.

It had been two months since she'd left Dr. Sinclair's company for the tech position at Sheffield's. The work had been challenging and fulfilling, yet she couldn't seem to keep her mind from slipping back to the simulator project—and the enigmatic scientist who'd designed it. *Careful, Jill. Dragons lie in that direction*. . . .

"I still think you're making a mistake," Marsha said, interrupting her thoughts. "I know you, Jillie. I remember back in graduate school, when you fought for every lost cause on campus. You even won a few. But this is different. This thing," she said, gesturing at the gigantic machine, "could get you killed."

Jillian gave Marsha a valiant smile, wishing she could do more to calm her friend's fears. But facts were facts. She knew as well as Marsha that there was a slight but very real chance that the neurocyber link established between the simulator and the human mind could rip a person's consciousness to shreds.

"Dammit, Marsh, you're making me nervous," Jill said, masking her distress with another bright smile. "I'll be fine, you'll see. It'll be . . . a piece of toast!"

"I hope you're right," Marsha commented, only slightly cheered by Jill's use of Einstein's favorite expression. "Look, I worked with E as closely as you did. That little computer means a lot to me too, but if you don't think you can go through with it, you back out. I mean it. Sinclair or no Sinclair, you back out."

"Count on it," Jill assured her. She started to say something else, but her words were drowned out by a ringing alarm. "That's the signal for unauthorized personnel to clear the area. Sorry, Marsh, but only techs—and victims—are allowed from here on out."

Marsha started to leave, but she turned back for a final word. "Remember what I said about backing out. This isn't worth your life. Besides, I need you," she added with a grin. "Kevin's bringing the whole engineering department to my party tonight, and you have to help me make a good impression."

"Like Kevin's gonna care," Jill called after her, grinning herself. Considering how besotted Kevin was with her beautiful Latino friend, Jill doubted he'd notice anyone else at the party. Or that Marsha would either, for that matter. Those two definitely had it bad for each other.

Jill started toward the Simulator, but her mind refused to stay focused on her project. The wires and steel scaffolding faded as she thought about Kevin and Marsha, and the special relationship blossoming between them. Jill was incredibly happy for her best friend, yet there was a small, secret part of her that died a little each time she saw them look at each other, their eyes shining with love.

Her thoughts ended abruptly as she ran full tilt into a man's solid chest. "Ohmigod!" she exclaimed.

Momentarily disoriented, she had a scant second to register the scrupulously spotless lab coat, the understated elegance of expensive cologne, the confident strength of hands on her upper arms, holding her with disconcerting gentleness.

"Steady on, Ms. Polanski. Are you all right?"

His rich British accent poured through her like sweet sunshine. Her gaze shot up, meeting the intense, deep-set eyes that never failed to stop her breath. Dark and broodingly handsome, he could have easily been mistaken for a matinee idol, the star of some torrid eighteenth-century melodrama set in the moors. His Lord Byron looks had set many hearts fluttering in the cyberengineering department, and he'd broken every one on his own heart of granite.

"I'm . . . okay."

"You should watch where you're going," he admonished her.

*Five seconds since we met and already he's giving me orders.* Nothing had changed. And yet . . . she thought she saw a flicker of amusement hovering near the corners of his stern mouth. And she could swear she detected an almost imperceptible softening in his steel-gray gaze. She swallowed, feeling unbalanced despite his anchoring hands. "Dr. Sinclair, I—"

A sudden shout distracted Jill. Reluctantly, she tore her gaze away from Sinclair's and glanced past his shoulder. Marsha was dashing toward her across the room.

"Jill, you forgot your gloves," Marsha called,

waving the bulky orange handgear. "You'd better not lose them, or your Dr. Doom will have your hide."

*My Dr. Doom*, Jill thought, wincing. She opened her mouth to explain, but Sinclair had already released his hold on her arms and stepped away. She looked up into his eyes and found them chillingly distant, like the space between the stars. The cold cut clear through to her bones. The warmth she'd thought she'd glimpsed a moment before had vanished—if it had ever been there at all.

"Here you go," Marsha said as she handed the gloves to Jillian. But even as she spoke her eyes strayed to the handsome, dark-haired scientist standing next to her friend. Being in love hadn't made her lose her appreciation for a good-looking man. "Who's the hunk?"

"Hunk?" Sinclair asked as a frown creased his forehead. "Hunk of what?"

"You don't know what hunk means?" Marsha said incredulously. She turned to Jill, nodding in Sinclair's direction. "Honey, we need to bring this man into the twentieth century. Make sure you bring him to the party tonight."

"Marsh, I don't think that's such a good—"

"Party starts at eight," she said, disregarding Jill's warning. Then, after delivering a final provocative wink at the doctor, she left the room.

Jillian knew Marsha hadn't meant to embarrass the hell out of her, but that didn't stop a telltale blush from creeping into her cheeks. "I'm sorry about that, Dr. Sinclair. Marsha doesn't know who you are."

"So I gather," he remarked dryly. "I doubt she would have invited *Dr. Doom* to her party."

"She wouldn't have called you that if she knew you," Jill said quickly, the words leaving her mouth before she realized how foolish they sounded. If Marsha had known Sinclair, she'd probably have called him much worse. In the five months Jill had worked with him, she'd never seen him laugh, or tell a joke, or show any trace of human feeling. Even the scientists and technicians who'd worked with him for years said that underneath his frosty exterior beat a heart of pure stainless steel.

And Jill had gotten more than her share of frostbite.

Okay, so maybe some of it was her fault. On her first day with his department she'd learned that the simulator waste products weren't being recycled properly. Environmental issues had always been her hot button, and when the doctor's secretary told her Sinclair couldn't see her that day, Jill had simply stormed into his office anyway. His cool gray eyes had met her fiery brown ones, and the battle was joined. For three months they'd argued about everything from environmental responsibility to simulator safety standards. They couldn't be in the same room for five minutes without fighting about something. Jill chalked up their battles to a deep-seated loathing for each other. Or she had, until the night of Harry Griffith's farewell party.

*Dragons . . .*

Sinclair checked his watch, then started a quick march toward the simulator without sparing so much as a glance in Jill's direction. "Step on it, Ms. Polanski. We're wasting time."

Jillian fell in behind him, noting the strength of his stride, the certainty of his confidence. Jill, whose life was a rabbit warren of human fears and failings, had been drawn to his self-assurance like a magnet to steel. Yet ultimately she'd been drawn by something even stronger—the flashes of emotion she'd glimpsed in his metal-hard eyes, the brief frowns of human uncertainty, the diamond-rare smiles. A champion of lost causes, she'd been incapable of turning her back on a man who appeared to be at war with himself.

But appearances, as always, were deceiving. Every attempt she'd made at friendship had met with at best renewed arguments, and at worst cruel indifference. The contradictions in his character had torn her apart like storm winds, ultimately coming to a head at Harry's party. She'd been dancing with several of her tech friends, when the music turned slow and intimate. She'd started to leave the floor, but suddenly, impossibly, found herself in Dr. Sinclair's arms, dancing to the sultry song.

At first courtesy kept her from pulling away, but courtesy was quickly eclipsed by a stronger and much more potent emotion. Sinclair's British heart may have been ice, but he danced with all the passion of a Latin lover. Jill let him lead her, meeting his passion with the forbidden feelings she'd kept locked inside, finally admitting to herself what she'd been fighting so hard to deny—that there was a man beneath the hard exterior, a man she'd been attracted to since the first time they'd met. Sighing, she lifted her gaze to his, opening herself emotionally in a way she hadn't done for years, and—drew back in shock at the look of cold, almost cruel interest in his eyes. He was studying her reaction, like one of his damn experiments.

Luckily, the song ended at that moment. She'd left the party and gone back to the safety of her home, feeling betrayed by his clinical curiosity, and by her own traitorous emotions. She'd gone to work the next day determined to put the episode behind her, but the moment she met Sinclair's cool gray gaze she'd felt the same potent attraction—and the same icy betrayal. And the more she tried to deny it, the stronger it became.

Jill wasn't a quitter. She kept up the farce for two months, stuffing down her unwanted emotions, trying to pretend that moment in his arms had never happened. But the effort took its toll, and the dishonesty began to sap her spirit. When she heard about the Sheffield cybertech job, she jumped at the chance, knowing it was the coward's way out, but taking it anyway.

Now her affection for Einstein had forced her back to Sinclair's side. *In his dire clutches,* she thought, smiling wryly at the melodramatic image. After all, this was a high-tech laboratory of the nineties, not some gloomy Yorkshire castle of the last century. And she could certainly keep her silly schoolgirl infatuation under control for the short time they'd be working together.

*Besides,* she thought as she looked over the doctor's head at the small "eggs" suspended in the center of the huge metallic scaffolding, *I've got plenty of other things to worry about.*


She was without a doubt the most uncooperative woman he had ever worked with.

"I don't care if you *wrote* the book on the simulator procedures," Sinclair said as he placed another self-affixing sensor on her temple. "You're going to listen to them again."

Jillian strained against the egg's bright yellow rayon-mesh harness, almost as if she were straining against his commands. "Haven't got much choice, have I? I'm a captive audience."

Logically Sinclair knew he should ignore her sarcasm just as he ignored everyone else's. Acknowledging slights was a waste of time in his opinion. It redirected one's mind and energy away from more important matters—like getting the job done. As a rule, both praise and insults rolled off him like water from a duck's back. But Jillian's comments stung.

Looking away, he reached behind him and picked up another sensor wire. The close quarters of the egg made it an uncomfortable maneuver, but Sinclair ignored the twinge of pain. Acknowledging physical discomfort was another waste of time. "When you first become 'immersed' in the virtual environment, you'll experience a minute or two of disorientation, like—"

"Like a sailor gaining his sea legs," she finished. "I *know*, Doctor. I've played Dactyl Nightmare and other virtual reality arcade games."

"So have I, Ms. Polanski, and those games are Tinker Toys compared with what you're about to experience. That's one reason I've limited a cybernaut's time to an hour in the simulated environment. After that, a person's higher reasoning skills begin to deteriorate—similar to a scuba diver's rapture of the deep. Now, after you become accustomed to the virtual surroundings, you'll see the power grid."

"The lines of light that map and stabilize the virtual world," she stated in a singsong voice.

His jaw tightened, caught between annoyance and admiration. She'd obviously studied the revised documentation carefully before returning, but why she had to repeat it to him in such an irritating manner . . . But then, Jillian Polanski had always been insubordinate. Insubordinate, argumentative, challenging, stimulating, exciting—

He cleared his throat in a loud harrumph. "They're more than just lines of light. They transmit energy units to the environment. If you cross one while you're in the virtual world they present no danger, but . . . do you recall what happens when a consciousness leaves the simulated environment?"

She reached down, apparently to tighten one of

the harness straps. "Yes," she said quietly. "The grid lines reenergize to full capacity. Anyone standing in one could receive a significant—possibly fatal— shock."

She continued to worry the harness strap. The low artificial light in the egg blurred the clarity of her profile, but Sinclair was a detail man, and the details of Ms. Polanski's features were something he'd made a study of more than once.

With scientific detachment he'd logged the fact that she was an attractive woman with a delicate, almost ethereal bone structure. Her smooth, soft skin was saved from bland perfection by a spray of freckles over a pert nose that another man might have called adorable. There was an energy about her, a vitality for life that others might have found stimu- lating, even intriguing. Bending nearer, Sinclair caught a whiff of the elusive scent that always sur- rounded her, a hauntingly familiar aroma that might have kept another man awake nights, that—truth- fully—had kept him up for a night or two since the evening of Griffith's party, when he'd held her body against his for that one, slow dance—

*Bloody hell!* He swore inwardly, clamping down on an image that had no place in his efficiently streamlined simulator, or in his efficiently stream- lined life. "This is not an arcade game, Ms. Polan- ski," he said, his voice a trace rougher than it had been before. "Once you're in the virtual environ- ment, everything you see, hear, touch, smell, and even taste will come to you through the computer.

The 'real world' will cease to exist. You'll be trusting your very sanity to the simulator."

"And to you," she added softly.

Her words unnerved him. He'd taken cybernauts into the simulator before—Dr. Miller, and at least a half-dozen others. Each of them had placed themselves in his hands, and he'd accepted that responsibility as part of his job. But as he stared into Jillian's wide brown eyes, that responsibility suddenly took on an awesome weight. Swaddled in Miller's hastily cut-down harness, she looked impossibly small, and fragile as a porcelain vase. For the first time the risks of the cybernaut seemed to outweigh the value of his research. For the first time, he hesitated.

"Ms. Polanski, you don't have to go through with this. We can find someone else, someone with more experience—"

"There isn't *time* to find someone else," she said with killing honesty. "Besides, I know this machine almost as well as you do. And I know Einstein like I know my own brother. There's no one more qualified than I am." She squared her shoulders and proudly pulled herself up to her full height, which was a good ten inches shorter than his own. "What's the matter? Don't you think I'm capable?"

Sinclair didn't get the chance to answer. A voice came over the egg's speaker, the familiar Brooklynese of senior technician Sadie Hedges. "Ready when you are, Doc."

"Doc?" Jillian remarked, smiling.

She had a beautiful smile. He'd noticed it from

the first—with clinical detachment, of course. It was one of the reasons she was so popular with her co-workers, along with her intelligence and forthright honesty. Jillian Polanski had the rare and invaluable gift of making other people feel important, and the project teams she worked on ran more smoothly and efficiently because of it. It was one of the reasons he'd regretted that she was no longer working for him.

A regret that was also due to the fact that he respected her technical skill and her intelligence, and secretly enjoyed their rousing arguments. It had absolutely nothing to do with the incredible dance they'd shared together. Nothing at all.

"I don't encourage nicknames, Ms. Polanski," he stated as he pressed the final sensor node to a spot on her jugular just below her ear. "Not from Dr. Hedges. Or from anyone else."

She blushed, and he knew she was remembering her friend's reference to Dr. Doom. Heat rose with her color, sweeping across the skin underneath his fingers to the pulse point at the side of her throat. Her warmth swept through his own body, shining through his inner darkness like a lighthouse beacon in the night. He jerked his hand away, startled and shaken by the unexpected warmth, the unwanted intimacy.

He pulled her display visor down over her face, cutting off her sight, and his view of her remarkably expressive eyes. Then he moved quickly to the door of the egg. "It will take me a few minutes to get into my own harness," he said more harshly than he intended. "Use the time to reacquaint yourself with the glove and visor controls."

"Dr. Sinclair?"

He paused at the egg's entrance, held fast by the poorly disguised uncertainty in her voice. She seemed so young, so impossibly unprepared to deal with the very real dangers of his invention. He gripped the side of the door, fighting an almost overwhelming urge to go back and rip her out of the harness and send her as far away from his simulator, and himself, as possible.

He didn't, of course. "Yes, Ms. Polanski?"

"I wanted you to know—" She hesitated, her brow furrowing in a rare frown as she searched for the right words. "Well, I just wanted to say that I'm not worried about entering the simulator. I know you won't let anything happen to me in there. I trust you."

*Trust.* Trust was an emotion unwise people assigned based on other fallible emotional reactions. Trust was something one decided not with the head, but with the heart—an unpredictable area of the body even at the best of times. He'd learned the hard way not to rely on anything that could not be documented, dissected, examined, or cross-checked. It would take something stronger than a pair of doe-brown eyes to make him forget it.

"You can trust whomever you please," he warned the young woman. "Just don't forget what the simu-

lator can do to you. Or that I am the one who created it."


*Toto, I don't think we're in Kansas anymore*, Jillian
thought as she opened her eyes and looked around.
She was surrounded by a relentlessly gray stillness,
like a thick bank of fog that was neither cold, nor
wet, nor . . . *anything*. The fog's eerie grayness
seemed more like the absence of color than a color
itself. The air seemed not so much silent as lacking
sound. The whole world seemed defined not by what
it was, but by what it was not. If nowhere was a
place, she'd found it. *Again*, she recalled with a
shiver.

Memories from almost twenty years ago surfaced
in her mind. Once again she was eight years old,
huddled in the corner of her tiny bedroom, covering
her ears to block out the living room shouting match
that centered, as usual, around her. As the volume of
her mother's and the latest boyfriend's fighting increased, Jill pulled her body into a tighter, smaller
ball and pressed herself into the hard angles of the
corner, pretending with all her childish heart that
she was in a place beyond the sound and anger, a
place where nothing existed, not even pain. . . .

"Ms. Polanski?"

She blinked, pulling herself out of the memory as
a person pulls off an old pair of boots. *You're in the
simulator*, she reminded herself. *And the long, lean
shadow standing beside you is Dr. Sinclair*. In the dim-

ness she could make out little more than his shape, a silhouette impression. Considering how easily her face betrayed her emotions, she hoped that was all he could see of her.

"Ms. Polanski, are you all right?"

She couldn't see his expression, but she heard the resonance of concern in his voice. Lord, was he actually worried about her? "Would it matter to you if I weren't?"

"Of course," he said brusquely. "If you experienced an adverse reaction to the simulator, it would jeopardize the mission."

"Naturally," Jill said dully. *Idiot!* She looked around, forcing herself to concentrate on her unusual surroundings. "Is this the inside of Einstein's computer?"

"It's the simulated environment of the inside of the computer," Sinclair corrected her. "Control, mark the time."

Before she could ask him how he expected her to accomplish this feat, another, more distant voice answered. "Time marked. Like you asked, I'll give you updates every ten minutes until the hour's up. Howya doing, Jill?"

"Fine," Jillian answered, recognizing the voice of Felix Parker, the boy wonder of the project. At twenty-three, Felix was already working on his Ph.D. in cyberphysics, but his sheer zaniness and puppy-dog friendliness prevented him from being classified as a computer nerd. He also didn't give a damn what people thought of him, a talent Jill had yet to master. "Hey, are you the one who came up with this oatmeal world?"

Felix laughed at her unflattering but accurate description. "Hang on, I'm firing up the topology program now. Dr. Sinclair asked me to come up with something a little more normal for your first time in the simulator. Wanted to make you feel more comfortable."

"He did?" Jill glanced up at the shadow man beside her, amazed that he would instruct his best engineer to basically "waste his time" on creating an environment designed to make her feel at ease. "You did?"

Sinclair didn't answer. He wasn't even listening. Instead, his dark profile showed that he was looking past her, at something beyond her shoulder. She turned around—and gasped.

Rolling toward them across the gray landscape was a tidal wave of color as wide as the horizon and as tall as the sky. Rainbow hues battled through its surface, a chaos of light and motion that was at once the most beautiful and most terrifying sight she'd ever seen. "God," she said in alarm, swinging her gaze back to her companion. "My God!"

"Don't worry. It can't hurt you." Then Sinclair did the strangest thing. He reached out and took her hand, holding it lightly in his own. Jillian knew he wasn't really touching her, that his hand was an illusion transmitted via the simulator to her mind's tactile nerve centers. But in an unfamiliar world with a huge, luminous wave bearing down on them at top speed, she found the human gesture incredibly comforting. She clung to his hand, drawing on his strength and reassurance. Then, raising her own head high, she turned back to face the wave.

Sinclair's prediction proved right, naturally—she barely felt the wave. It passed over her with only a slight tingle, like the brush of a wayward breeze. But it left behind an entire world.

Suddenly she stood in a field of waist-high wildflowers vaulted by a heaven so radiantly blue, it seemed to shine with its own light. A stand of tall laurel trees stood off to her left, proud as sentinels, dressed in all the brilliant pageantry of full summer. Beyond them lay a tangled forest, a patchwork of greens so varied, they seemed to be an entire rainbow in themselves. And beyond the forest lay a tranquil valley dotted with neat houses and even hedgerows, simmering in the easy laziness of the late afternoon.

Jill took a deep breath of the sweet-smelling air, awed to silence by the incredible change in her surroundings. The simulator environment was real beyond belief! She raised her free hand to shield her eyes from the bright sun, and discovered yet another surprise. Her surroundings were not the only things that had been transformed by the wave.

Her black bodysuit was gone, replaced by a gown of ivory velvet, its puffed sleeves cut with panels of silver and gold. Seed pearls decorated an edge of her bodice, continuing in an exquisite vine-and-leaf pattern from her high-waisted torso all the way down her long, flowing skirt. She'd never imagined that a dress could be so beautiful, and gasped again, this time in appreciation and wonder.

Her wonder was cut short by a sharp oath spoken beside her. "Bloody hell, Parker's put us in a Dungeons and Dragons game!"

*Good Lord, he has,* she thought, smiling at Felix's irrepressible sense of humor. He'd bugged her for weeks to play D & D with him, but Jill had told him truthfully that she didn't have the time. Apparently her friend had made her a player in spite of herself. She turned to the doctor to explain Felix's little joke, but the words froze in her throat.

She was staring up at the gleaming helmet of a knight in shining armor.

# TWO

There had been a time in Sinclair's life when he would have given anything to wear a suit of armor like this—even a virtual one. As a boy he'd read every book about King Arthur he could lay his hands on, even braving the dusty stacks of his grandfather's ancient library to find them. More than once he'd received a caning for taking what he later learned was a shockingly valuable volume, but that didn't stop him. Reading was his greatest pleasure during the years he'd spent living in his grandfather's elegant mausoleum of a manor house. Sometimes his only pleasure, considering he was the sole child on the immense, isolated estate.

He'd devoured the stories of the Round Table, imagining himself riding alongside those knights, vanquishing villains, slaying dragons, and rescuing damsels in distress. They were wonderful dreams, but he'd paid dearly for every one of them. He'd become a knight of sorts, but the title had proved to be as empty as the suits of armor that lined the manor's cavernous hallways. And rescuing a damsel in distress had nearly cost him his soul.

"Bloody hell," he cursed again, but this time he wasn't thinking about Parker's environment. He shoved up his visor—his *virtual* visor, since it, like everything else, was merely a projection from his simulator—and swung his gaze to the woman beside him. "Ms. Polanski, we have only an hour, so we'd better get star—"

The rest of his sentence dwindled into oblivion. Ms. Polanski had disappeared. In her place stood a fairy princess garbed in white and crowned with a circlet of gold. Strands of light brown hair blew across her cheeks, making his fingers itch to follow their course. Her low-cut neckline revealed a tantalizing view of the swell of her breasts, filling his inquiring mind with theories that had nothing to do with the simulator or his mission. Dragging his gaze upward, he ran into more trouble when he focused on the exquisite delicacy of her petal-soft skin, and the unconscious sensuality of her ripe, flower-shaped mouth. A mouth like that could love a man a hundred ways, and make him beg for a hundred more. Childhood dreams crashed headlong into erotic adult fantasies.

"Bloody hell," he breathed for the third time in less than a minute. "Ms. Polanski, you look—"

"Fifty minutes left," a disembodied voice boomed.

Parker's announcement shattered the moment. Sinclair stiffened, all too aware that he'd narrowly missed making a complete ass of himself. He turned away, inwardly cursing his foolishness, and ruthlessly reminding himself that this world, and everything in it, was an illusion. The sun-drenched pastoral landscape that surrounded him wasn't real. The supernatural beauty of the woman who stood at his side wasn't real. In a sense, *he* wasn't real.

But the stab of regret he felt was, unfortunately, very real. "We should get moving."

"Yes . . . yes, we should."

She sounded breathless, uncertain. He frowned, wondering what she had to be uncertain about. Then he remembered that it was her first time in the simulator, and probably as strange to her as Alice's first trip through the looking-glass. He glanced back at her, willing himself to see beyond the fairy princess to the nervous cybertech beneath. "Don't worry, Ms. Polanski. Chances are we won't see a large white rabbit with a stopwatch hopping by."

"I was more concerned about the Wicked Witch," she replied, giving him a shaky smile.

Her clothes may have been an illusion, but her smile was not. He'd seen it before—analyzed it, catalogued it, and determined what use it could be to him in his work. But he'd never realized the effect it could have on a man. Deep inside him a buried longing stirred to life. He hadn't felt this way about a woman in years, not since Samantha—

Samantha!

He spun around, ruthlessly severing the fragile bond that had begun to form between them. "Come," he commanded harshly. "We're wasting time." He stalked through the field, his heavy steps indifferently crushing the delicate flowers into oblivion. Virtual flowers, he reminded himself. This place was an illusion, a projection designed to make internal navigation easier. Life and death were properties of the real world, along with duty and honor and all the other truths he'd been taught to believe in.

Truths, he'd discovered, that were as false as the bright and counterfeit flowers beneath his boots.


"Twenty minutes left," Parker announced.

"Damn," Jillian fumed as she attempted to tug her skirt free from yet another snagging bramble. Her beautiful outfit was a disaster when it came to cross-country travel—the heavy material seemed almost magnetically drawn to every thorn in the vicinity. More than once she'd been tempted to shuck the elegant but unwieldy gown and go on without it, but she didn't dare. She knew Felix was a stickler for detail—the unpleasantly real bramble bushes proved it—but she doubted whether even he had thought to include a pair of virtual lingerie in his topological design.

She felt ridiculous! She gave her skirt another frustrated yank, trying to ignore the embarrassed blush that heated her neck and cheeks. "Dr. Sinclair, you go on. If we split up, we can cover more territory."

The doctor stood a few yards away from her on a small cairn of stones, scanning the unexplored part of the valley. He barely glanced back in her direction as he answered, "That's not advisable."

Jill started to ask exactly what was advisable, but Sinclair had already turned his back on her, returning his gaze to the valley as if she didn't matter at all. Correction—*because* she didn't matter at all. She meant less to him than the bluebottle that buzzed around his helmet in the still afternoon air. A fly that wasn't even real.

Sinclair may have looked the part of a brave and chivalrous knight, but underneath the shining armor he was as cold and heartless as he'd always been. Saving Einstein meant nothing to him—and she meant even less than nothing. It was like reliving the humiliation of their slow dance all over again.

Anger built within her, only this time her frustration had little to do with her skirt or the brambles. "You don't give a damn, do you?"

Sinclair looked back at her. "What did you say?"

"I said *you don't give a damn,*" Jill repeated, her anger increasing with every carefully enunciated word. "This is just another experiment to you. You don't care whether we save Einstein or not."

"Ms. Polanski, I assure you that finding the computer is my highest priority."

"Highest priority," she repeated acidly. "Doctor, Einstein isn't a priority, he's a *person*. He's the kindest, sweetest, most wonderful personality I've ever met—and that includes the people I know. He's my friend—one of my best friends—and I'm not about to give up on him because we're not meeting some . . . arbitrary rules you've established." She raised her chin and gave him what she hoped was a grandly haughty stare. "I don't care what you say. I'm going off on my own so we double our chances of finding E, and that's *final.*"

Jill gave her skirt a sharp yank, hoping to pull it free and make a glorious exit. Unfortunately, her dress wouldn't cooperate. No matter how hard she pulled, she remained firmly anchored in the bramble bush. In fact, her frantic tugging only seemed to make matters worse.

"It would appear," Sinclair commented dryly, "that you're not going anywhere."

*Damn him*, she thought. *Damn his blue-blood smile and his superior attitude.* Anger from a lifetime of injustice boiled up inside her, bringing sharp tears to her eyes. People like him had made her childhood a living hell. Words from the past whispered through her mind, names that still had the power to wound her, even after all these years. *Gretchen Polanski's little problem. That unfortunate Polanski girl.* And the worst of all, *Gretchen's mistake.* "Go ahead and make fun of me," she told him bitterly. "I don't care."

For a moment he remained perfectly still, carved, it seemed, from the stones he stood on. Then he bent his head and slowly, deliberately, removed his helmet.

Jill's traitorous heart constricted in her chest. Bareheaded, with his usually immaculate hair tousled into a dark tangle, the doctor looked more impossibly handsome than ever. She felt a sudden urge to run her fingers through those curls, a quick, foolish image that opened a Pandora's box of other desires. Dammit, she was supposed to be angry with the man!

"Ms. Polanski, my *arbitrary* rules are designed to save your pretty little—" He paused, his eyes narrowing as he gave her figure a bold once-over before adding, ". . . neck. I require cybernauts to stay together because there's always a chance a person's reasoning won't last the full hour . . . not to mention the other hundred things that could endanger someone whose mind is linked to a synthetic environment."

He started to walk toward her, his slow, deliberate movements making her silently add another danger to the ones he'd already mentioned. Lord, maybe her reason *was* beginning to deteriorate. Otherwise, how could she explain the crazy images that flashed through her mind—of her, and him, doing . . . oh, Lord! She closed her eyes, shutting out his advancing figure, knowing instinctively that she had to get away—fast. She twisted around, struggling so violently against the brambles that they began to tear the material.

"Jillian, keep still."

Sinclair? It couldn't be. She'd never heard him sound so gentle, so patient. She opened her eyes, slowly at first, then finished with a wide stare of disbelief. Sinclair knelt before her, painstakingly unhooking her velvet dress from the hundred angry prickers. His touch was as gentle as his words.

Jill's wonder was quickly eclipsed by horror. "Dr. Sinclair, you shouldn't . . . I mean, you don't have to—"

"Help you?" he said, glancing up at her with his wry grin. "I suppose it does go against my Dr. Doom image." He finished pulling away the thorns, then rose to his feet and held out his hand to assist her out of the bush. "We'll just keep this between ourselves, shall we?"

Swallowing her apprehension, she placed her hand in his. Warm fingers clasped her own, reminding her of the other time he'd held her, at Griffith's party. She recalled the humiliation, but somehow that stern, cold-eyed stranger seemed less real than the virtual man who stood beside her.

"Thanks," she said shakily, attempting to put her feelings into words. "I didn't expect you to be so . . . good at untangling skirts."

Sinclair's dark brows arched up in a humor that did not reach his eyes. "I suspect that's a compliment. Thank you."

The edge of self-deprecation in his voice stabbed her heart. *It's not real,* she told herself. Dr. Sinclair had a hide of iron and a heart to match. Yet as she looked into the depths of his eyes, she caught a glimpse of the soul behind his stainless-steel personality, a soul as uncertain and easily wounded as her own. It was probably an illusion, as counterfeit as his gleaming armor and his jewel-encrusted sword. Yet, illusion or not, his gaze captured her, drawing her in like a wandering comet caught in the gravitational pull of the sun.

Forces far stronger than her human will closed like a fist around her heart. The virtual world faded, leaving only his questioning eyes and her over-whelming need to answer those questions. Stepping closer, she brushed her fingers gently against his cheek. His eyes darkened at the slight caress, the hard silver turning molten at her touch. She felt the heat of his gaze quicken in her own body. *Illusion*, her reason warned. Yet in the deepest, truest part of her, she knew that this was the most real thing she'd ever felt in her life—

"Ten minutes," Parker warned.

Jill's hand dropped to her side, her common sense rushing back like air into a vacuum. It had happened again! She'd let herself be seduced by the image of the man she wanted Sinclair to be, rather than seeing him for the cold fish he was. She turned away, unable to face the cool calculation she knew she'd find in his eyes. "We'd better get moving. We haven't got much—"

"Ms. Polanski?"

"Yes?" she replied, pretending to be fascinated by a stand of trees off to the left.

The doctor hesitated, then cleared his throat. "Harrumph. Yes, well, I just wanted to make you aware that the simulator's representations of . . .

certain responses, can be digitally corrupted. You shouldn't be overly concerned by what happens here. It's . . . only a projection."

Jill stiffened. Was Sinclair actually trying to make her feel less foolish about what she'd done? Or was he just setting her up for another experiment? She turned back, meeting the doctor's gaze with open suspicion. But before she could determine his intent, he frowned and looked past her, fixing his gaze on the stand of trees she'd recently pretended to study.

"There's something moving behind those poplars."

"Do you think it's Einstein?"

"Maybe," he said, walking past her. "But I'd advise you to stay behind me all the same. There's no telling what might be over there."

He started toward the trees, but Jill called him back. "Dr. Sinclair? I just wanted to say . . . well, thanks. From one projection to another."

He glanced over his shoulder, arching his eyebrow in wry amusement. He started to say something, but he never got the opportunity. At that moment the "something" came out from behind the concealing trees.

It wasn't Einstein.

The creature was huge with gray-green skin and arms as thick as tree trunks. It walked upright and wore a dirt-caked leather tunic, but those were its only concessions to humanity. Bloodred eyes glowed malevolently from under its jutting brow, and over-size yellow canines curved up from its lantern jaw. Worst of all, the thing smelled as if it hadn't had a bath since Creation.

"Good Lord!" Sinclair exclaimed, stopping dead in his tracks. "What is that thing?"

"I think it's an orc," Jillian said as she came to his side. "A small one."

"*Small?*" Sinclair swung his gaze back to the advancing monster. Slightly stooped, it still stood well over seven feet. It looked as if it could wrestle a baby elephant to the ground—with one arm tied behind its back.

And it was heading straight for them.

"Parker!" Sinclair barked. "Get that thing out of here!"

"I'm trying," Felix answered, "but the pattern's imbedded in the topological matrix. I can't locate it."

"Bloody hell," Sinclair cursed, finding the oath more useful as time went by. The topological program listing for this overlay was easily six inches deep. Unless he knew exactly where to look, Felix wasn't going to find the creature's pattern anytime soon.

Sinclair shook his head, feeling the beginning of a tremendous headache coming on. He glanced back at the giant monstrosity, grateful that the ponderous thing moved slowly. They could easily outrun it. He grabbed Ms. Polanski's wrist and started back the way they came, intending to do just that.

Ms. Polanski didn't budge. "Uh-oh," she said.

*Uh-oh* proved to be an understatement. Looking back, Sinclair saw that his cybernaut partner had inadvertently stepped right into the middle of another bramble bush. Slow as the monster was, it would reach them before they could free her from the thorns. Sighing, he realized there was only one solution. "Cancel the experiment, Hedges. Bring us out."

There was a long silence before Sadie Hedges's disembodied voice answered him. "I can and I can't, Doc."

"Sadie," Sinclair breathed, trying to contain his temper, "this isn't open to debate. Bring us out. *Now!*"

"Doc, *you* I can bring out, no problem. But look where *she's* standing."

Sinclair peered through the tangle of branches at his partner's feet, and saw a faint flickering line of cobalt blue. Damn. The thorn bush was situated right on top of one of the lines of the power grid. And Ms. Polanski's shapely ankle was far too close to it for comfort. Sinclair's headache began to throb in earnest. "Well," he said as he raised his hand to the jeweled sword, "it appears I'm going to get a chance to see if virtual armor holds up like the real thing."

This time it was Ms. Polanski's hand that closed around his wrist. "Doctor, it's just a projection, right? It can't really hurt you."

Sinclair looked into her earnest eyes. Gently, he

lifted her hand from his arm, exhibiting the same care he'd used to untangle her dress from the prickers. "I designed the simulator to emulate physical stimuli," he told her calmly, as if he were commenting on the weather. "*All* physical stimuli."

Yards off, the plodding monster roared, as if acknowledging his statement. *Damn*, Sinclair thought as he glanced at the creature, *the thing looks like a Sherman tank on legs.*

"I won't let you do this!"

He swung his gaze back to his fellow cybernaut. Bedraggled, with her gold circlet askew and her elaborate dress ripped and ruined by a hundred grasping prickers, she stood with her head high, her brown eyes flashing with absurd but somehow effective pride.

"Forgive me, Ms. Polanski, but you're hardly in a position to dictate to anyone."

"I'm not dictating. I'm using my head," she stated, crossing her arms resolutely in front of her. "You can leave. I can't. You're the brains behind this operation, not me." She raised her chin, meeting his gaze without a trace of fear. "You're not expendable, Doctor. I am. Leave me your sword, and get out while you can."

Sinclair looked at her, amazed and impressed by the courage and the clarity of her logic. Earlier something had passed between them, something she could have traded on if she'd wanted to. But not her. Backed to a wall, he imagined she'd go down fighting rather than beg for even an ounce of mercy. Some people ran from adversity, others met it head-on.

Sinclair suspected that Jillian Polanski was one of those rare individuals who could have had adversity for lunch.

"That's . . . excellent reasoning."

"Then you'll go?"

"No, but it's a fine argument. Now, if you'll excuse me, I have an appointment with a walking bulldozer."

"Doctor, I . . ."

Her sentence dwindled away, leaving behind a silence that said more than words ever could. Bright tears shimmered in her eyes, tears of fright, but not for herself. Deep inside him, something cracked open.

He remembered the moment they'd shared not ten minutes before, the tenderness he'd denied, labeling it as a glitch in the simulator program. Complicated feelings were often corrupted by the black and white logic of the simulator matrix. But that didn't stop him from being drawn to the emotions he saw in her eyes. Nor did it stop him from remembering the touch of her hand against his cheek—soft as silk, and gentle in a way he'd almost forgotten how to want. *Lord, who am I kidding? I wanted to dance with her at Griffith's party. I practically sprinted across the room when that slow song began. . . .*

Jillian licked her lips—a simple process that had a

nuclear effect on Sinclair's abdomen—and spoke again. "Doctor, I don't even know your first name."

"It's Ian," he said as he turned around to face the advancing monster. "And just for the record, Ms. Polanski, you're not exactly what I expected either."

# THREE

Sinclair had braved danger in the name of science before. When he was eleven he'd blown up his grandfather's prize rose garden in an experiment that successfully illustrated the combustible qualities of fertilizer. During his first year of graduate school an accident with an overzealous cyclotron had landed him in the hospital for a month. Dying was a calculated risk in his line of work, and Sinclair had prepared for the possibility with the same conscientious thoroughness he practiced in the rest of his affairs. He'd drawn up a will, and updated it on a quarterly basis. He'd made sure that his technicians and assistants were familiar with the body of his research so that his work would go on. He had no reason to regret the possibility of dying—except for the somewhat unscientific desire to want to go on living.

As the orc lumbered toward him, Ian began to think about all the things he hadn't done, the theories he hadn't tried, and the words he hadn't said to Partridge, the only person he'd allowed himself to care about. Other thoughts came to mind as well, like the seductive innocence of Miss Polanski's smile, and the tantalizing glimpse he'd gotten of her long, shapely legs. No, he definitely did not want to die at this particular moment.

As he looked up at the orc's massive shoulders and his demon-bright eyes, however, Ian conceded he might not have much choice in the matter.

"Parker, any luck getting rid of this thing?" he called.

"I'm trying," Felix answered, sounding harried. "It's not that easy."

*It's a damn sight easier than standing in front of the bloody thing.* "All right, just do your best," he said as he sent up a silent prayer that Parker's best would be good enough. And his. Because if he couldn't stop this creature before Jillian got free of the brambles and power grid, his neck wasn't going to be the only one on the line.

"Bloody hell," he growled, advancing toward the creature with the caution of a dog approaching a baited bull. He drew his sword from its scabbard, taking heart in the clean whisper of steel against steel. Holding it aloft, he tested its balance, instinctively assessing the weight and character of the blade. When Ian was a child, his grandfather had demanded that he be trained in the broadsword, a tradition in the Sinclair family that stretched back to the 1600s. Ian had fought against learning it, just as

he'd fought against learning all the seemingly senseless traditions that added to the suffocating weight of
his heritage. But at the moment he was grateful for
this one. "All right, you walking garbage scow," he
cried in challenge. "Let's see how you fair against
good English steel."

The orc roared, and answered Ian's challenge
with a swipe of his massive paw. Ian ducked, easily
avoiding the monster's slower movements. The creature had size on its side, but Ian had speed, and he
intended to use it. He lunged forward in a move that
would have made his old fencing master proud, and
nicked the orc's arm above the elbow.

The beast let out a tremendous howl, knocking
Ian backward with the sheer force of the sound.

"Ian, be careful!" Jillian cried from behind him.

Unable to resist, he stole a look over his shoulder. She stood arrow-straight in the twisted brambles, her chin held high in a stance of magnificent
defiance. Yet her brave posture couldn't completely
hide the quiver in her lips and the fear in her impossibly wide eyes. Once again their gazes locked, and
the strange, molten magic began to flow between
them. She was the loveliest thing he'd ever seen, a
genuine damsel in distress. Only her distress wasn't
for herself, but for him.

Parker broke the spell. "Doctor, is anything
wrong? Your body temperature just jumped ten de-
grees."

*Felix boy, you have a beautiful woman look at you like
this and see what happens to your temperature.* "I'm

fine," he said curtly, reluctantly pulling his gaze away from Jillian.

He was still partially turned toward her when the orc's swipe caught him on the side of his head, toppling him end over end down the slight slope. When he came to rest, his helmet was gone, knocked off by the force of the blow. From the stabbing pain in his neck, Sinclair suspected that his head had tried to go with it.

He sat up, rubbing his aching temples, and tried to shake some sense back into his thundering skull. Well, he thought with a grim smile, at least his virtual reality simulator was a success. These aches and pains felt *damn* real. He looked up, expecting to see the orc lumbering down the hill after him.

But the orc wasn't following him. Someone was distracting it by throwing rocks at its hairy hide. Someone with no virtual armor to protect her, who'd suffer more than aches and pains if the monster got his paws on her.

Ian leapt to his feet, ignoring his strained muscles as he pounded up the slope. "Jillie, for God's sake, *stop!*"

The stone she was about to throw dropped unheeded to the ground at her feet. "You're alive," she cried, a radiant smile lighting her face. "Ian, you're alive!"

He felt the warmth of that smile blaze within him, and die a moment later when the orc, after a second's confused hesitation, continued to lumber toward Jillian. Anchored in place by the brambles, she was a sitting duck for the approaching monster. In the real world her body was safe, protected from physical danger in the cybernaut's egg. But her mind was tied to this virtual environment by the simulator, and Ian knew that if she was wounded in this world, her consciousness would mirror the injury in the real one. Even a fatal injury.

He ran up the slope, fear adding speed to his steps. He paused only once to retrieve his fallen sword, but never took his gaze off the creature. Despite its ponderous bulk, it had managed to make its way almost within striking distance of Jillian. She'd balled her hands into fists and raised them like a boxer in a ring. *She's insane*, whispered a voice in Ian's mind. *She's extraordinary*, whispered another.

Blood sang in his veins. Ancient instincts rose within him, passed down from ancestors who had fought barbarians, kings, and dictators to protect those who could not defend themselves. *Agincourt. Waterloo. Dunkirk.* Names of legendary battles sprang to mind, legacies of a heritage swaddled too long in musty traditions and recycled glories. It was time to reclaim his birthright.

Ian raised his sword and yelled a war cry bred into him before he took his first breath. The unexpected sound distracted the orc, who swung its hoary head away from Jillian toward the charging knight. It stared at Ian, its lips twisting into a parody of a smile. Slowly, the orc drew back its massive arm to deliver a final death blow.

But Ian struck first. Ignoring the danger, he ran

full tilt into the deadly circle of the giant's arms and, with both hands, plunged his sword into its heart. The creature's scream shook the world. Arms flailing, it caught Ian square in the chest, and sent him flying several yards through the air. Then the beast collapsed to the ground, its noxious green blood spilling out around its body.

Ian sat up gingerly, wincing at the discomfort even this simple movement caused. Every muscle in his body burned like hellfire, but it didn't matter. He'd won. He'd stopped the bastard before it could touch her. She was safe.

The orc remained in a crumpled pile, Ian's sword still planted in its heart. He wiped his hand over his face, feeling strangely light-headed. Thoughts began to fade in and out of his mind like a badly focused movie. He remembered vaguely that there was a very important reason he'd challenged the monster. He just couldn't recall precisely what it was.

"Dr. Sinclair, please say something!"

Like a man in a dream, he turned to the woman kneeling beside him. Ms. Polanski, his mind supplied. The beautiful Ms. Polanski. And at that particular moment the rather scantily clad Ms. Polanski. Her elegant gown was shredded almost beyond recognition, the remaining velvet forming the first and probably last medieval microskirt.

"I left most of the dress behind in the thorn bush," she said, following the direction of his gaze. Self-consciously, she raised her hand to push back a strand of her tangled, bramble-snagged hair. "I guess I look pretty awful."

Awful? She looked bloody marvelous. Her brown hair framed her head in a wild halo, making her look like a wood nymph, a creature of legend. But the rest of her was decidedly human. The ripped and ragged dress gave him a first-class view of her slim waist, her graceful arms, and a pair of legs that seemed to go on forever. Ian swallowed, feeling a burning in his gut that had nothing to do with his sore muscles.

"Dr. Sinclair? Ian?"

His name had never sounded so sweet. He lifted his gaze, noting the distress in her wide brown eyes. *Wood nymph. Forest creature.* He recalled his victory, the battle he'd fought to save her, but that wasn't what he was trying so hard to remember. It wasn't until his gaze drifted down to her petal-shaped lips that he recalled what he wanted to do, what he'd *been* wanting to do for what seemed an eternity. *A mouth that could love a man a hundred ways, and make him beg for a hundred more . . .*

Without a word he reached out and folded her into his arms, determined to try at least one.


*This isn't happening,* Jillian thought in panic as his mouth closed over hers. The simulator had gotten some wires crossed. Dr. Sinclair wouldn't kiss her. And if he did, his kiss wouldn't send pure sunshine shooting through her veins. . . .

During the last few minutes Jill had lived a lifetime's worth of emotions, her feelings careening wildly from horrified helplessness to transcendent joy. Trapped by the brambles, she'd watched Sinclair's seemingly lifeless body tumble down the hillside, knowing there wasn't a thing she could do to help him. A pain she'd never felt before pierced her heart. Nearly choking on tears of rage, she'd turned her fury on the orc, pelting him with stones that didn't even dent his leathery hide. She didn't give a damn about her safety—she didn't give a damn about anything at the time.

But nothing—not her horror, despair, or joy—came close to the intensity of the emotions blazing through her now.

"Jillie," he whispered.

He said her name again, but this time he murmured it against her mouth, stroking her with the double assault of his warm breath and his hot, questing tongue. He dipped between her parted lips like a bee tasting a flower, wooing her with the delicacy of the act. She just—just—managed to survive the gentle seduction. Until he did it again.

*Lord, what am I doing?* she thought wretchedly. This was Sinclair, the man who had a stopwatch for a heart. She tried to pull away, but he held her fast, his steel strength more than living up to his metallic image. She opened her mouth to protest, and found herself invaded by the hottest, wettest kiss she'd ever received. He sampled her deeply, his rough tongue making lazy, erotic swirls that turned her blood to slow, hot honey, and her heart to a pounding jackhammer. *I shouldn't be doing this*, she thought again, but this time the intentions behind the words were considerably weaker, like smoke dissipated by the wind.

Hands that should have pushed him away pulled him closer, seeking out the soft, dark curls at the nape of his neck. Soft and strong, steel and fire—his contradictory textures fascinated her. Common sense sieved from her mind like sand through an hourglass, leaving room for something bright and burning, something too wonderful to be captured by a name. His kiss poured colors into the lonely gray corners of her soul: sunburst yellows, shimmering greens, enchanted blues, and ruby desires. Every stroke of his tongue gave her another piece of the rainbow.

His hands drifted down, his long fingers spanning all but a few inches of her narrow waist. He pulled her hips against his, gently molding their still-clothed bodies into a more serious embrace. She surrendered eagerly, knowing that a part of her had been waiting all her life for his caress, his spellbinding, kaleidoscope embrace. Instinctively their bodies began to move together in the beginning of a love dance. *Love.*

She arched closer, filled with his magic, aching with the need to make that same magic happen in him. She mated her own tongue with his, and his moan of pleasure shivered through her like a hundred tiny explosions. *This is real*, she thought as the joy of pleasing him erupted through her. *God, please make this be real.*

Her silent plea went unheeded. One moment she was locked in his arms—a heartbeat later she wasn't. Fingers that she'd knit into his soft, dark curls clutched emptiness. Lips that were hot and throbbing from the hunger of his kiss felt the cool brush of climate-controlled air. She felt the tiny pressure of the sensors on her body, heard the muted click of calibrated monitors as their circuits opened and shut. Pushing up her visor, she stared at the equipment-studded interior of the egg, feeling empty, and cold, and more alone than she'd ever been in her life. "No," she whispered helplessly. "Oh, no."

The egg's door whooshed open, admitting a stream of stinging light and the angular form of Sadie Hedges. "Boy, kiddo, you had us scared. We thought we'd lost you."

Jill blinked her eyes at the sudden light, feeling disoriented and cheated. "Where's . . . Ian?"

"Still trussed up like a chicken, I imagine," Sadie said cheerfully as she hunkered down to unfasten Jill's harness. "The doc told me before you went in that he wanted me to get you out first, since this was your first time in the simulator's cyberspace."

Simulator? Cyberspace? They were two words in a crossword-puzzle consciousness that still had a lot of letters missing. Jillian passed her hand over her eyes, feeling more confused than ever. "Don't remember . . ."

"You will," Sadie assured her. "It'll take you a

minute to get your bearings, especially since you were in the simulator almost seven minutes over the recommended limit." She pulled back Jill's harness, and started to remove the sensor nodes from her skin and bodysuit. "Just open your mind and let the memories come back to you at their own speed. It won't take long."

Sadie was right. As soon as Jill stopped trying, the memories flooded into her mind like a movie on rewind. She remembered the orc, the snagging brambles, the wonder of the sunny summer world and the gray emptiness preceding it. She remembered the gleam of armor and the flash of a sword, and the enchanted embrace of a knight who'd risked his life to save her. She remembered the passion, the pleasure, the multicolored magic that had bound them together like two halves of the same heart. Despair replaced wonder as she realized it had all been an illusion, a beautiful dream that had never happened. And horror replaced despair as she realized that real or not, she still had to deal with the consequences.

*She'd kissed Dr. Doom!*

Jill struggled against the remaining restraints like a wild bird caught in a huntsman's net, her gloved, still-uncoordinated fingers fumbling helplessly with the harness's clasps. "Sadie, get me out of this thing!"

"Hey, where's the fire?" joked the older woman, extracting the clasp from Jill's death grip. "No need to panic. You're safe."

Safe? She'd never felt more *unsafe* in her life. She needed to get away, to find a quiet corner where she could come to grips with what had happened, where she could compose herself . . . hell, where she could *hide*. She was no coward, but the thought of facing Dr. Sinclair after the ecstasy she'd just experienced—correction: which she'd thought she'd just experienced—in his arms, was enough to make anyone run like a rabbit. "Just get me out," she said, closing her eyes as a wave of embarrassment washed over her. "Please."

Sadie frowned in concern, but she did as Jillian asked. In another minute Jill bolted out of the egg and down the steel ladder that connected the simulator's higher levels to the ground. She reached the floor and started toward the far door at a fast clip, wanting to put as much distance as she could between herself, the infernal machine, and the equally infernal man who'd created it. She pulled off her stiff DataGloves with a vicious tug, and wiped a lone tear from her cheek. *Tears of anger*, she assured herself. *I'll be damned if I'm going to cry over losing a knight in shining armor who wasn't even real to begin with.*

"Ms. Polanski!" called an all-too-familiar voice behind her.

*Sinclair.* He must have gotten himself out of his harness without waiting for Sadie's help. Jill hunched her shoulders and kept on walking, pretending she didn't hear him. With any luck, she'd make the door before he caught up with her.

But luck, as usual, wasn't with her. Before she'd

taken ten steps, Dr. Sinclair was beside her, his long legs making short work of the distance between them. "Ms. Polanski, just where do you think you're going?"

*Somewhere you're not*, she thought, purposely continuing to look straight ahead. Not that it did much good. She could feel him beside her, the lengthy, lean form of the man who had—and hadn't—saved her life. Angry anew, she shoved her hands into her pockets, her ire increasing tenfold as she realized her bodysuit didn't have any pockets. "What's it to you?" she bit out. "Our search for Einstein is over until tomorrow. I'm leaving."

"I can't allow that. We need to discuss the events that transpired during our time in the simulator, to log them in with the rest of my research and test results."

*In your dreams, Doctor.* She wasn't about to discuss what had *transpired*, with him or anyone else on God's green earth. Hell, she intended to do her best to forget it! She glanced up ahead of her, noting that the laboratory's door—and freedom—were less than ten yards away. "We'll talk about it tomorrow."

"We'll talk about it *now*, Ms. Polanski."

He stepped directly in front of her, effectively cutting off her escape route. Firm hands grasped her shoulders, barely preventing her from running into him for the second time that day. Only this time there were two distinct differences.

The first was that he wasn't wearing his lab coat. Like her, he was still dressed in the simulator's "immersion" suit, and the dark, form-fitting material carved the planes and angles of his body with the precision of a sculpture's chisel. She saw the ridged muscles of his chest, the understated strength of his lean hips and powerful legs. With a shock, she realized that his voluminous lab coat had concealed the classic lines of a body so perfect, it would have put Michelangelo's *David* to shame. The man was muscle and sinew from head to toe. No wonder he'd beaten the orc.

The second difference was her point of view. The downward direction of her gaze afforded her a first-class look at a part of his anatomy that gave a whole new meaning to the word *perfection*. The black bodysuit left little of his form to her imagination, and at the moment her imagination was working overtime. *Strong fingers capturing her waist, holding her against him as they moved in unison to the rhythm of their beating hearts. . . .*

Her head shot up. Her gaze collided with his, and registered the presence of something undefinable moving in the depths of his silver eyes. But the look was gone before she could identify it, his glittering metallic sharpness back in place. She swallowed, suddenly feeling as if she were the orc, facing down the tempered steel of his blade. "Please," she said weakly. "I'm tired. Can't we do this tomorrow?"

Her voice pleaded for mercy. His eyes gave her none. He studied her with the same fascination she'd seen him use to examine logarithmic equations, absorbing the difficult problems into himself until they had no choice but to yield up their secrets. Unfortunately, she wasn't an equation, and the bold intensity of his gaze robbed the air from her lungs and made her personal parts ache with almost unbearable longing. Custer had more chance of surviving Little Big Horn than she did of surviving that look. She tried to back away, physically retreating from the onslaught of his piercing gaze. His hands held her fast.

"Please," she begged. "Let me go."

At that moment Felix rushed toward them, a ream of computer paper trailing behind him. "Dr. Sinclair," he cried enthusiastically, "I think I've figured out how to get rid of the orc!"

Distracted, the doctor glanced toward Parker. His grip slacked almost imperceptibly, but it was enough for Jill to slip out of his grasp and sprint out of the room. She was halfway down the hall before she turned around to see if he'd followed her, and experienced a crazy jumble of relief and disappointment when she discovered he hadn't.

*Well, what did you expect? A mad dash after you and a confession of undying devotion? You're a guinea pig to him, Polanski. Handle it.*

And as she continued down the corridor, that's exactly what she did. She dealt with her difficult emotions as she'd handled them since she was a child, stuffing them deep into the empty corners of her soul, finding more than enough room. It was just her tough luck that she had to displace a few rainbows to do it.

❖————————————————❖

"He kissed you?" Marsha asked in open-mouthed surprise. "The hunk kissed you?"

"Dr. Sinclair kissed me," Jill replied sternly. She raised her elbow and shoved an unruly stand of hair off her forehead, then continued to chop the salad tomatoes into needlessly small pieces. "But it wasn't a real kiss. It happened while we were in the simulator."

Marsha gave a snort of disbelief. "Honey, let me set you straight," she said as she dumped another handful of mushrooms into the salad. "Lip lock is lip lock, whether it happens here, there, or on the moon. It's the action that matters, not the location. So," she asked slyly, "how was it?"

Jill was spared from answering by the unexpected arrival of Kevin, who blew through the kitchen door like a brawny, red-haired hurricane. "Hey, you guys have been in here forever. Want some help?"

Jill had seen Kevin helping in the kitchen, and it wasn't a pretty sight. He was one of Sheffield Industries' most experienced computer hardware engineers, but he didn't know a Cuisinart from a spatula. Anyway, she suspected his unexpected appearance had more to do with Marsha's presence than with his desire to help. Ten minutes appeared to be the limit on how long he could stand to have his lady love out of his sight.

"We'll be out in a minute, snoochems," Marsha

assured him. Apparently satisfied, Kevin lumbered out of the room.

"Snoochems?" Jill said, staring at her friend in amused disbelief.

"Hey, guys love it," Marsha answered in self-defense. "And know what? Kevin told me there's about four guys in the other room who would love it if you called one of them snoochems."

"Get real," Jill replied, all too conscious of her less-than-devastating looks. With her short brown hair and brown eyes, she thought she was about as scintillating as the wheat fields surrounding the Nebraska town where she'd been raised. She looked at Marsha's exotic Latin looks with a twinge of envy. "They should stamp MIDWESTERN FARM GIRL on my forehead and turn me out in mass production."

"You always underestimate yourself," Marsha complained. "I'll bet Dr. Doom would love it if you called him snoochems."

"You'd lose big-time," Jill promised as much to herself as her friend. "Besides, Sinclair is the kind of guy who likes women's minds. Preferably when they're in small glass jars soaking in formaldehyde."

"Now you're underestimating your doctor," Marsha said as she hoisted the sizable salad bowl.

"He's not *my* doctor," Jill argued, scooping up the tomatoes and dumping them into Marsha's bowl. "Anyway, you'd better get that out to *snoochems* before he and his buddies start to eat the furniture. I'll wait for the pizza."

"Thanks," Marsha replied as she opened her eyes

wide in humorous fear for her furniture. She headed for the door, but turned back just as she reached it. "You know, Jillie, you really do underestimate yourself. Someday that's going to get you in trouble."

*You're wrong*, Jill answered silently as her friend left the kitchen. The trouble she'd gotten into had come from *overestimating* herself, from forgetting who she was. Or *what* she was. She still remembered the snickers, the hissing whispers from the other students as the secret of her parentage rippled through the senior prom crowd. One remark—one spiteful remark—and a night that should have been a shining dream shattered into a nightmare ruin. She'd been on the stage when it happened, being crowned prom queen of Middleton County High School. She could still recall the dwindling voices, the halfhearted applause, the way even her best friends couldn't manage to meet her eyes. She stood in the bright spotlight in a stainless white dress, and she'd never felt dirtier in her life.

She'd prayed God would strike her dead on the spot so she wouldn't have to face the condemnation, disappointment, and especially the pity of the friends she'd given her heart to. But God hadn't heard her . . . any more than he'd heard her that afternoon as she walked away from the simulator.

She leaned against the refrigerator and pressed her hands to the aching tightness between her breasts, wondering if it was possible to die from embarrassment. A scholarship to MIT had allowed her to escape the first time. A job at Sheffield Industries had allowed her to escape the second time, when she'd developed that ridiculously one-sided crush on the handsome doctor. But she doubted she'd get that lucky a third time. Tomorrow she'd have to face Sinclair and discuss their kiss—a kiss she'd enjoyed a whole lot more than she cared to admit. He'd log her private, precious emotions in his test data, using her like a human guinea pig. Maybe she should have left him to that orc after all.

A knock sounded on the back door. *Great, at least I can drown my sorrows in pepperoni.* She grabbed her purse and started to dig through it for her wallet, which was down at the bottom as usual. Grumbling fiercely, she opened the back door, her head still bent as she pursued her contrary billfold. "I'll have your money in a minute. Just put it on the table."

"I'd be happy to, Ms. Polanski, if you'd tell me what *it* you're referring to."

Jill's purse thumped to the floor. Her eyes shot up, meeting the glittering gaze of Dr. Ian Sinclair—scientist, orc slayer, and the man who'd done more damage to her self-respect than anyone since high school.

And the bastard was smiling.

# FOUR

"Wh-what are you doing here?" Jill stammered.

"I was invited," Sinclair replied simply, his infuriating smile deepening. In one smooth movement he reached down and retrieved her purse, handing it to her as gallantly as if he were delivering a nosegay. "Don't you remember, Ms. Polanski?"

Jill clutched her bulky purse to her chest like a shield. She remembered all right—that, and a great deal more. Though he was dressed casually, in black jeans and a loose midnight-blue shirt that emphasized his dark, brooding face, she couldn't help remembering the way he'd looked in a suit of shining armor. Memories came flooding back with devastating force. She recalled the strength of his arms, the gentle seduction of his hands, the impossible rightness of the way their bodies moved together, his heat, his taste . . .

"I remember," she said, her words sounding

more like a croak than the forceful statement she'd hoped for. "But you hardly ever come to parties."

He fixed her with his silver gaze. "I came to this one," he said softly, "because I wanted to see you."

"Oh," she said weakly, her purse again dropping to the floor. Her leaden arms had lost the strength to hold anything. Horribly she realized her knees weren't far behind. *He came because he wanted to see me. . . .*

"I wanted to see you," he continued as he again bent down to collect her fallen purse, "because you left the lab before we had a chance to discuss and log what happened in the simulator."

Discuss and log . . . He'd come here to add her to his test results. The man didn't even have the decency to wait until the next day! Furious, Jill spun around and stalked across the kitchen, heading for the living room door. But before she reached it, Marsha entered from the other side with Kevin in tow.

"Jill, somebody rang the front doorbell but they left before—Dr. Sinclair!"

Any hope Jill might have cherished about Marsha's support died as she watched her friend catch sight of the handsome scientist. With a coquettish toss of her hair and a thousand-watt smile, Marsha went straight into flirt mode.

"I'm so glad you could make it," she said, ushering Sinclair into the kitchen. "By the way, sorry about that nickname crack I made earlier. No offense meant."

"None taken, Miss Valdez. In fact," he added with the ghost of a smile, "I found it eminently appropriate."

*Good God, he's got a sense of humor*, Jill thought in distress. "Dr. Sinclair won't be staying long," she said hurriedly. "He just needs some information about our experience in his simulator and—"

"The virtual reality simulator?" Kevin exclaimed, his eyes growing big as saucers. "You're *that* Sinclair?"

Ian gave a low chuckle. "Dr. Doom in the flesh," he assured the goggle-eyed engineer.

After that, things got complicated. Kevin, and most of the rest of his engineering department, appeared to be card-carrying members of the Dr. Ian Sinclair fan club. Once they entered the living room, Marsha's party guests swamped the scientist with a barrage of technical questions and a wave of unabashed admiration. Jill expected the doctor to be annoyed by the attention, but to her surprise he handled the group with ease. He even—unbelievably—appeared to be enjoying himself.

He gave every question his full attention, and answered every compliment with an apparently sincere thank-you. His earnestness was as compelling as his knowledge. By the end of the evening he had everyone in the room eating out of his hand. Everyone, that is, except Jill.

She sat in a distant corner, munching cold pizza, feeling very confused. She'd known Dr. Sinclair for months, and he'd never displayed one tenth of the animation he was exhibiting tonight. She didn't get it. Ice cubes had more warmth than the Ian Sinclair she knew. She wondered if he had a twin brother, a personable man who'd temporarily taken the place of the enigmatic scientist. Or maybe it was just she who brought out his cold and unfeeling side.

But he'd kissed her . . .

No, he hadn't, she reminded herself sternly. He'd kissed a woman in cyberspace, a projection, a phantom. He'd never held her in his arms, never thrilled her with his touch, never consumed her with the seductive glory of his caress. Worse, he wanted to dissect the non-event for his research notes, reducing her tumultuous feelings to a series of passionless test results. Well, maybe he could fool the others into thinking he was a decent, caring human being, but she knew better. And if he thought she was going to bear her soul to him like some well-trained lab rat, he had another think com—

"Ms. Polanski? Are you all right?"

Jillian opened her eyes and looked up into the molten silver eyes of the courageous knight who'd saved her from the orc. She reminded herself the knight wasn't real, and neither was the counterfeit concern in his gaze. "I'm fine," she stated sharply. "Why wouldn't I be?"

"I have no idea, but you've been holding that piece of pizza in front of you a full minute." He leaned closer, smiling gently. "We were beginning to worry."

"Worry?" Jill repeated, caught off guard by the

soft humor in his expression. She'd always thought of Sinclair as a hard man—whether as a steel-skinned scientist or an armor-garbed knight. Softness didn't figure into her image of him. Yet, as she looked at him for once without anger, she noticed the small laugh lines at the corners of his eyes, and the way his mouth turned up when it was hovering toward a smile. She knew from her experience in the simulator what it felt like to kiss him, but she suddenly found herself wondering what it would be like to laugh with him.

*Right, Jill. Yet another emotion he can dissect.*

She glanced away from the doctor, her gaze seeking out Marsha. "I'm a little tired. I . . . think I'll just go on home."

"I'll drive you," Sinclair decided, apparently not caring that she was no longer looking at him.

"It's not necessary. I live only a few blocks up the beach. I'll just walk."

"Then I'll walk with you," he said as he extracted the half-eaten pizza from her hands.

The brief touch of his fingers, firm, warm, and decidedly unmetallic, made her realize how close she was to letting herself feel something more than infatuation for this man. Walking alone with him on a deserted beach wasn't even close to being a wise choice, yet she found her protests weakening. "Well, if you really want to . . ."

"I most certainly do," he stated as he helped her to her feet. "It will give us a chance to discuss what happened today in the simulator."

❖─────────────────❖

The few blocks to Jillian Polanski's house were some of the longest Ian had ever traveled in his life. They walked along the beach in the North Miami suburb, listening to the hush of the night waves and the intermittent blare of a far-off channel horn. The night was warm, even balmy, despite its mid-winter calendar date. Yet Ian felt a definite chill in the air— a chill radiating from the woman who walked beside him.

"We're almost at my house, Doctor," she said curtly. "Ask your questions. What do you want to know?"

He glanced at her, noticing her bent head and hunched shoulders. The woman was definitely on the defensive. She reminded him of a box turtle he'd had as a boy, a cautious creature that was forever disappearing into its shell. Every time the animal retreated, Ian felt as if he'd done something wrong, as if he'd failed it in some inexplicable way.

If Miss Polanski had a shell, he doubted he'd ever see her face. Dammit, why was she so wary of him? "What I'd like to know," he said honestly, "is why you are so dead set against discussing what happened in the simulator. Dr. Miller never minded."

"Well, Dr. Miller didn't . . . I mean, you never . . . look, I don't see why you need my input anyway. You were there—why don't you just write down your experiences?"

"Because that's what they are—*my* experiences.

It's important that I know your experiences too. I'd like to know what you thought and felt."

"Why?"

The simple question hit him broadside. His step faltered, though he told himself he'd tripped on a piece of driftwood. "Because we're scientists, Ms. Polanski. Because we're pioneers in the field of virtual reality, and it's our duty to log our results so others will be able to build on our work and avoid our mistakes. Perhaps our experiences will help save the life of another scientist. Surely you agree with that."

"Yes," she said softly. "I do. I wouldn't want to jeopardize anyone's safety. You're right, Dr. Sinclair."

She spoke his name dully, as if all the life had been sapped right out of her. Unbidden, his mind called up an image from their time in the simulator, when she'd knelt beside him in her provocative travesty of a dress, saying his name. *Ian.* Simulator or no simulator, his body still reacted to the sweet, enticing memory.

He turned his head toward her, noting that she'd sunk her fists into her jeans pockets, hunching her shoulders again in a posture so guarded, it put his box turtle to shame. Darkness curled around her, making her look small and vulnerable, and achingly young.

"We're not going into the simulator tomorrow," he said suddenly. "It's been a hard day and we could both use some rest."

"But Einstein—"

"Einstein will have to wait. I'm not risking my equipment—or your life—by pushing you too hard."

"I don't need to be coddled," she snapped.

*Very much like my turtle.* "I never imagined you did. I remember how you fired off that barrage of stones at the orc. No one with an arm like yours needs to be coddled."

She smiled. It was a hesitant, ungainly grin that lasted less than a second, yet it managed to set his heart tumbling in his chest. Something very close to sympathy tugged at his heart. "Why don't you want to talk about what happened in the simulator?" he asked again.

For a moment she didn't answer. Then she sighed, a sound as soft and forlorn as a night breeze. "I don't want to end up as a footnote in some musty science journal, or as a point of illustration in your lecture notes. What happened to me in the simulator was very—special. Reducing it to a series of test results seems . . . I don't know, like killing the golden goose."

Sinclair wanted to tell her she was being foolish, but he couldn't get the words out. As a scientist he'd killed more than his share of golden geese. Taking things apart to see what made them tick was his business, even if that meant gutting them of their beauty and mystery as well. The discipline had bled over into his personal life. He recalled how often Samantha had accused him of practicing it in their marriage. What she hadn't accepted was that their "golden" union had been nothing more than dross from the beginning.

His smile turned brittle. "My wife used to say golden goose was my favorite meal."

Jillian came to an abrupt standstill. "You're married?"

"*Was* married," Ian amended, still walking. "It ended a year ago, but I suppose old habits are hard to break."

"I'm sorry," Jill said as she caught up with him.

*I'm sorry*. He'd heard those two words a hundred times, and had learned to hate them. During their marriage, pretty, petulant Samantha had prefaced almost all her sentences with it, especially when she was asking for forgiveness, or money. He'd indulged her in both for far too long. Now, of course, she didn't bother. She just had her lawyer send his lawyer another demand.

Intellectually he knew Jillian had meant to be kind, and that she couldn't possibly know the loathsome memories associated with those particular words. Nevertheless he spoke to her with more harshness than he intended. "There's nothing to be sorry about. I was raised by my grandfather as an only child. Being alone suits me. Besides, it gives me more time to spend on my—"

It took him a moment to realize she was no longer walking beside him. Turning around, he saw she'd stopped in her tracks.

"We're here," she said simply, nodding toward the modest town house that fronted the beach.

It was just the sort of place he expected her to live in. A floodlight illuminated the back of the house, showing its cheerful cornflower-blue siding and neat white trim, and the window boxes stuffed with colorful flowers. The condominium's small back deck was all but enveloped by a jungle of houseplants, and a set of wind chimes picked merry, tuneless notes from the night breeze. The town house looked crazy, chaotic, and welcoming in a way no home of his ever had. He turned his gaze toward the ocean's darkness, feeling as if he'd been robbed of something he couldn't begin to name. "Well then, good night, Miss Polanski. I'll call you tomor—"

"You can stay."

Sinclair spun back so quickly, he almost lost his balance on the loose sand. "What?"

"For coffee, I mean." She shifted from foot to foot, nearly losing balance herself. "It was kind of you to walk me home. I just wanted to . . . oh, hell, it was a stupid idea. Forget it."

Without waiting for his answer, she started up the slope of the beach to her condominium. Shoulders back, chin tilted toward the stars, she reminded him of another woman, a fairy princess with a slipping gold circlet, pelting a ferocious beast with ineffectual stones. Warning voices cautioned him not to accept her offer, that her cheery little house might hold greater dangers than any ferocious orc. Yet before he knew it, he was beside her, shortening his stride to match hers. "Coffee is fine, but I would prefer a cup of tea. Earl Grey, if you have it."

"I think I can find a bag." She smiled again, the tentative grin that had such an arresting effect on his heart. Once more the warning voices sounded, telling him that he was veering from his meticulously charted course and heading straight for unmapped waters. He shrugged off his misgivings, reminding himself that he was a respected scientist who lived a strict, disciplined, and completely satisfactory life. He was no callow youth to be ruled by the hormonal urges of his body.

And Ms. Polanski, the voices added, was no box turtle.

"Tell me, Ms. Polanski," Sinclair said as he studied the Save the Whales poster hanging over her living room couch, "are there any causes you don't support?"

"One or two," Jillian acknowledged with a slight smile. She set the tea tray down on the coffee table and glanced around the room, noting the wildlife photographs and the framed certificates of achievement she'd earned from the Sierra Club. The room was stuffed with memorabilia of battles she'd fought for those who could not fight for themselves. She was proud of every inch of it, but she could see where it might be overwhelming to someone who wasn't expecting it. She picked up the manatee-shaped mug from the tray and handed it to the doctor. "Some of my friends think I go a little overboard with my conservation efforts."

"If more people went overboard, our planet would be a better place in which to live." He lifted his mug to take a sip, but paused as he noticed its unusual shape. Sinclair glanced back at her, arching his dark brow in wry amusement. "Then again, your friends may have a point."

Jill laughed, a warm, bright sound that held almost as much surprise as humor. She'd invited Sinclair in on an impulse, reacting instinctively to the edge of desolation she'd heard in his voice when he'd mentioned his divorce. But now that he was here, she found herself enjoying his company. She hadn't expected him to be so interested in her conservation efforts. She appreciated his intelligent questions and his insightful remarks. But she was honest enough with herself to admit those weren't the only things she enjoyed.

By anyone's standards, Dr. Sinclair was an incredibly handsome man. Whatever she felt about him personally, he was one great-looking hunk of humanity, and she saw nothing wrong with a little surreptitious perusal. She settled on the couch and picked up her panda-shaped mug, taking a long, unhurried sip as she watched him move around the eclectic jumble of her living room. Lord, the guy even *strolled* sexily. . . .

"Bloody hell!"

Jill straightened up so quickly she almost spilled her tea. For an embarrassing moment she thought he'd caught her ogling him. Then she realized that his ire was focused not on her, but at the fat and fluffy black Persian cat at his feet. Jillie couldn't suppress a delighted chuckle. "Ah. I see you've met Merlin, my refugee from the humane society."

Ian glared at the creature. "He doesn't look like a refugee. In fact, he looks bloody pleased with himself. I could have broken my neck."

Merlin glared right back at the doctor, his leisurely waving tail indicating that he couldn't have cared less.

Jill watched the stalemate with profound enjoyment. She'd never seen Dr. Sinclair so perplexed before—even the bloodthirsty orc hadn't ruffled his trademark reserve the way her stubborn little cat had. *Dr. Doom meets his match*, she thought, smiling broadly. She was tempted to leave them there all night, but, as her grandparents would say, that wouldn't be the Christian thing to do. Besides, she owed the doctor a rescue.

She got up, walked over to the stubborn pair, and scooped up the fluffy assailant. "Merlin, you're a devil," she scolded as she scratched the cat's chin. "I'm sorry, Doctor. I should have warned you that Merlin rules the roost around here."

"I don't think he likes me," Ian remarked sullenly.

"That's just because he doesn't know you," Jill replied, strangely reluctant to let the doctor believe he'd been snubbed. "Just scratch him under the chin like this, and he'll be your friend forever."

Ian frowned suspiciously. Nevertheless, he reached out and gave the cat's chin a tentative scratch. It was an amateur effort, but Merlin didn't seem to mind. His great golden eyes drifted shut, and he began to purr with a vengeance.

"You see, he *does* like you," Jill said as she glanced up at the doctor. "He just needed to know that—"

Her words died on her tongue. Ian was grinning at the cat—a wide, lopsided grin that shone with boyish pleasure. It was the first honest smile she'd ever seen on his face, and it hit her with the force of a sucker punch. *Careful, Jill, you've been fooled by him before. Remember, you're his experiment. He thinks of you as a guinea pig, or a lab rat. Don't get fooled again.*

Bending down, she deposited the mollified Merlin on the carpet and walked stiffly back to the couch. "You wanted to discuss the simulator," she reminded him as she sat down. "Ask away."

Ian gave the cat a final pat, then walked over to sit on the opposite end of the couch. His frown returned. "You do seem tired, Ms. Polanski. If you'd rather, we can discuss this tomorrow."

"We'll discuss it now," she said, crossing her arms in front of her. "I want to get this over with."

A wry smile pulled at the corners of Sinclair's mouth. "You know, I get the distinct impression you'd rather face an orc than talk about what happened in the simulator today." He rested his elbow on the back of the couch and propped his chin on his fist, studying her with undivided interest. "Why is that?"

Damn him! His intense, absorbing gaze cut through to her heart, searching out her intimate secrets without exhibiting a trace of emotion himself. A surgeon wielding a scalpel couldn't have been more masterful—or more cruel. She felt alone and vulnerable, and unexpectedly, horribly aroused. "I didn't ask to be part of your experiment," she said quietly. "I volunteered because I wanted to help Einstein—period. I'm not doing this for the sake of science, or to help mankind."

For a moment he said nothing, but his jaw pulled into a tight line, and his eyes hardened to a hard, metallic sheen. When he did finally speak, it was with chilling, brittle politeness. "Forgive me, Ms. Polanski. I hadn't realized how much I was presuming on your charitable nature. I'll—how did you put it?—get this over with as soon as possible."

He pulled a small pad from his pocket and made a few quick notations. "Normally I'd ask you to chronologically relate your experiences in the simulator, but that would take hours. Suppose we just attempt to recreate the events of the virtual world in the real one? Dr. Miller and I regularly perform this exercise. Once I ran ten miles to replicate the feeling of climbing a virtual mountain. Another time I bungee-jumped off a bridge to—"

"*You* bungee-jumped?" Jill asked, astonished.

"For the sake of science, yes," he informed her stuffily. "I'm asking you to do the same. Are you up to it?"

"To go bungee-jumping?"

"No, no. To recreating one of the events you experienced in the simulator."

Jill shrugged. "I guess so, but I don't see how. I don't exactly have a suit of armor stored away in my closet."

"I was thinking of something a little more prosaic." He put down his notepad and leaned closer, absorbing her once again with his silver gaze. The corners of his stern mouth twitched up, but there was nothing humorous in his smile. "I'm referring to the kiss, Ms. Polanski. I think we should recreate the kiss."

# FIVE

Jill shot up from the couch and stared at Ian in open-mouthed amazement. "You've got to be kidding!"

"Not at all," Ian assured her, wondering how she'd managed to divine humor from his perfectly logical request. Perhaps he hadn't made himself clear. "Of all the events we experienced in the virtual world, the kiss would be the easiest to replicate. You see—"

"Oh, I see, all right," she said, propping her hands on her hips. "I invite you in for tea—just tea—and you try to grab some extra dessert."

"What dessert?" Ian asked, now thoroughly confused. "You never offered me dessert."

"Damn straight I didn't," Jill agreed, her brown eyes wide with fury. "I was wondering why you were so interested in my environmental work. Now I see why. You thought that by buttering me up, and then giving me some song and dance about your simulator, you could cop a quick one. Well, I'm not that kind of woman, Dr. Sinclair." She bent to the table and snatched up the manatee and panda mugs, gathering them in her arms as if to protect them from his touch. "If you're so keen on *replicating our experience*, you can just go and kiss Dr. Miller!"

Her terse remarks about Dr. Miller finally clued Ian in as to what she was thinking—though how she could have reached *that* conclusion from his sensible suggestion was beyond him. "Ms. Polanski, you can't actually imagine that I *want* to kiss you?"

Instead of comforting her, his remark seemed to upset her even more. Without a word she spun around and headed for the kitchen.

*Bloody hell, what have I said now?* Ian wondered as he rose from the couch and followed her. He stood in the doorway, watching her carefully set the animal mugs in the sink and turn on the water. Unaccountably, he found his gaze straying to her hands, studying their unconsciously graceful movements, and the delicate care she bestowed even on those silly little mugs. It was so like her to treat the small and unimportant things of the world with profound respect. Mugs, manatees, stray cats—they all received her caring attention. But not well-intentioned yet ill-spoken scientists.

He cleared his throat, suddenly feeling as awkward as a teenager. "Ms. Polanski, I'm not good at expressing myself. I never have been. But if I offended you in any way, I'm truly sor—"

"It's not true."

For a moment he thought she meant his apology. "Excuse me?"

"It's not true," she repeated softly as she continued to wash the mugs. "I don't know how much you've heard about my background, but what you're thinking about me isn't true."

Bent over the sink, he couldn't see her expression. But the defeated slant of her shoulders told him more than her words ever could. Ian didn't consider himself a sympathetic man, but the weariness, the isolation in her posture, touched him deeply. He'd spent a good portion of his life alone, and knew how wearing it could be on the spirit. But until that moment he'd never thought of popular, outspoken Jillian as ever feeling lonely or unsure of herself.

"Ms. Polanski," he answered in a tone as hushed as hers, "the only thing I'm thinking is that I haven't the faintest idea of what you're talking about. Which appears," he added with the ghost of a grin, "to be the rule rather than the exception for this evening."

She glanced back at him, her brown eyes as wary as a skittish doe's. He recalled the last minutes they'd spent in cyberspace, when she had come to his side in that tattered dress with her hair full of brambles, smelling of loam and moss. He'd thought of her as a wood nymph, a fairy creature of spirit and fire, a dream never to be recaptured. Yet now, right in the mundane world of soap suds and coffee mugs, he again found himself staring into the eyes of that wood nymph—or eyes that would have belonged to a wood nymph if they hadn't been clouded by suspicion and distrust.

Something twisted near his heart. For all her causes and courageous stances, Jillian Polanski was as delicate as lace inside. Sinclair had seen how cruel the world could be to fragile and unique spirits, but he'd never seen a pair of eyes more tragic or a spirit more afraid to let its true nature be discovered. He wondered who had taught her to be so wary, and experienced a surge of anger so strong, it nearly made him wince.

"I'm sorry," he said hoarsely, wondering whose damage he was apologizing for. "I never intended to hurt you."

She studied him for a few moments longer. Then her mouth sneaked up in a tentative half-grin that made his heart twist all over again. "I'm sorry too. I shouldn't have jumped to the conclusion that you were after something." She turned back to the sink and finished rinsing the mugs. "I mean, everyone knows you never think about anything but science."

*Not always, Ms. Polanski.* As Dr. Doom he'd fostered a reputation for stoic indifference. But underneath his passionless exterior beat the heart of a normal, red-blooded man with all the normal, red-blooded desires as the rest of his race. Nowadays he tried to ignore that part of himself—letting his heart rule his head had almost ruined his life. Still, his physical self kept asserting itself, usually at inconvenient moments. Like during the slow dance at Griffith's party. Like now. Try as he might, he couldn't stop staring at Ms. Polanski's petal-shaped mouth, and thinking some distinctly unscientific thoughts.

When they'd come out of the simulator, the shock of reentering the real world had wiped the details of their kiss from his mind. He recalled the event visually, like a silent movie, but the additional sensations of sound, touch, and taste were missing from his personal memory banks. He'd lost partial sensation memory of other cyberspace events before, but he'd never regretted the loss so keenly.

Until that moment he'd never questioned his motives for asking Jillian to help him recreate their kiss. But gazing at her soft, inviting lips, he had the uncomfortable suspicion that there might be more to his suggestion than he'd realized. After what he'd glimpsed in her eyes a moment earlier, he didn't want to give her yet another reason for not trusting someone. Perhaps it was a lucky thing she'd turned him down after all.

"Okay," she said suddenly.

"Okay what?"

"Okay, I'll kiss you."

Ian stared at her dumbfounded. For a second he thought he was back in the simulator, and Parker had switched realities on him while he wasn't looking. "But you just said—"

"I *know* what I said," she replied as she picked up a dish towel and wiped her hands, "but I figure you're right about it being for the good of science. Besides, if I don't, I'll always wonder if what I felt in the simulator was . . . well, I'll just always wonder.

Anyway," she added with a shrug, "it's only a lousy kiss."

Lousy? *Lousy!* Ian's recollection of their kiss may have been hazy, but he was quite sure it deserved a better modifier than that one. He remembered enjoying it. He remembered *her* enjoying it. His disastrous marriage to Samantha had destroyed much of his belief in himself, both as a scientist and as a man. But nothing in this world or the virtual one would ever convince him that the kiss he'd given Jillian Polanski in cyberspace had been anything less than first class.

A determination he hadn't felt in years welled up inside him. Quick as thought, he reached out and captured Jillian's wrist, pulling her against him. He took a thorough, satisfied look at her wide eyes and wonderfully shocked expression, then turned to the kitchen door, pulling her after him.

"Hey!" she cried, finally finding her voice. "What do you think you're doing?"

"Taking you back to your living room," he explained simply. "It's the most logical place to replicate the cyberevent." But logic was only half the reason. Simulator or no simulator, he intended to kiss Ms. Polanski until her toes curled.

Then see if she called it "lousy."


Jill expected the doctor to give her a quick, perfunctory kiss, jot a few lines down in his notebook, and be done with it. But, as usual, Dr. Sinclair didn't behave at all as she expected. Instead of kissing her immediately, he led her slowly into the living room. Once there, he let go of her wrist and started to pace the perimeter of the room with the taut energy of a caged panther.

Jill rubbed her wrist, torn between anger and confusion at his sudden change in attitude. One minute he was staring at her with a look so intense, it stole her breath. The next, he left her standing on her own as if he'd completely forgotten her existence. Irritated, she propped her hands on her hips, not even attempting to hide her annoyance. "Tell me, Doctor, do you treat all the women you intend to kiss this way?"

Sinclair glanced at her over his shoulder, flashing her a cocky grin. "And why do you want to know about the women I've kissed, Ms. Polanski?"

"I don't. I—" Jill's speech sputtered out, choked off by anger and indignation. Honestly, the man was infuriating! "I just want to know what you're doing."

"Well, why didn't you say so?" He stopped pacing and turned to face her, still wearing that infernal grin. "I was examining the room for possible visual matches with the simulator environment, something we could use to help recreate the cyberspace world. But there doesn't appear to be anything—not unless you've got a bramble bush or a mountain meadow stashed in your closet."

"I might have an orc," she said dryly.

Ian chuckled, a warm sound that poured through her like fine brandy. "I think I'll pass on that suggestion. However, since the visual aspect of the experiment is a dead loss, the best thing we can do is to block it out. Removing our visual input will heighten our other senses."

"Fine. I'll close my eyes," Jill said, wanting to get on with it.

"That's one solution," Ian agreed. "But I think I have a better one." He bent down to the lamp on the end table beside the couch and switched it off.

Jill's irritation crystallized into sharp panic. She hurried over to the lamp and switched it back on. "I'd rather close my eyes."

Ian's dark brows arched in amusement. "Very well, I accept your alternate solution—this time." Still smiling, he settled his long, lean frame onto her couch, and nodded to the cushion next to him. "Shall we begin?"

Jill's body suddenly seemed to be made of melted wax. Her knees gave way and she sank down beside him, though farther away than he'd indicated. All at once the room seemed blisteringly hot, and so stuffy that she found it difficult to breathe. *It's just a kiss. One stupid kiss* . . .

Yet in her heart she knew it was much, much more.

In her own way she was as determined as Ian to recreate the simulator event—but her reasons were very different from his. The doctor wanted to prove that their virtual kiss was identical to a real one. She, on the other hand, wanted desperately to prove that it wasn't.

Try as she might, she couldn't drive the memory of his kiss from her mind. She recalled every detail, from the searing touch of his fingers to the intoxicating taste of his lips. And the colors—oh, glory, she couldn't help but remember the colors he'd made inside her. But the most indelible detail of all was the completeness she'd felt when she was in his arms, the uncanny sense of absolute rightness that had happened when his lips molded to hers. His kiss was a beautiful, magical experience—almost too beautiful to be real. Too beautiful, certainly, to be created by the dispassionate Dr. Doom.

As a child she'd lived in a world of dreams, using make-believe to shield herself against the painful realities of her everyday existence. But now she was an adult, and she could not allow herself to be consumed by foolish fantasies—especially fantasies that centered on a man who had a microprocessor for a heart. Dr. Sinclair's "rainbow" kiss was an illusion created by crossed circuits and faulty diodes of the simulator, and she had to shatter that illusion before it took hold of her life.

She closed her eyes, glad now that the doctor had requested she do so. It made everything seem much less personal. Taking a deep breath, she leaned forward and offered up her tightly pursed lips.

"I'm afraid that won't do, Ms. Polanski."

Her eyes snapped open. "Why not?" she demanded with growing annoyance. "A kiss is a kiss."

"But it's not a *replicated* kiss," he explained. "In the simulator we were sitting . . . closer."

Closer? They were practically on top of each other! "Look, I agreed to kiss you, but this is getting out of—"

"What's the matter?" he asked, his eyes glittering with dark amusement. "Afraid?"

*Hell, yes,* Jillie thought. But she wasn't going to let him know that. She'd never backed down from a challenge in her life, and she wasn't about to start now. Stiffly, determinedly, she moved into his arms, willing herself to ignore the unexpected gentleness of his hands, and the frantic thumping of her own traitorous heart. She squinched her eyes shut, using the physical movement to help her shut off her chaotic inner emotions. She could bear it for a moment, just long enough for the doctor to kiss her and prove that the virtual kiss wasn't anything like a real one.

Just long enough to wash away her bright rainbow dreams into gray and dreary puddles.


Ian rarely made mistakes. He considered them the province of other people, negligent people who did not do their research and consequently reached miscalculations. But the moment he took the reluctant Ms. Polanski into his arms and lowered his mouth to hers, he knew he'd made one of those infrequent mistakes. And—in the words of Partridge's Americanized vocabulary—it was a *whopper*.

He felt the tension in her body, the rigid fatalism of a person approaching a firing squad. Judging by her physical reaction, he suspected that she'd rather kiss an orc than him. He paused a millimeter above her lips, sobered by the thought that he'd manipulated her into this position with all the heartless cunning of his former wife. No experiment was worth that. Ashamed, he started to draw back, when the soft, warm whisper of her breath brushed his lips.

And suddenly honor meant nothing. Justice meant nothing. The desire he'd thought long dead rose within him like a slumbering giant, waking with a silent roar of triumph. Arms he no longer controlled tightened around her. The mouth he'd thought to apologize with descended on hers like an eagle falling on its prey. Rivers of passion, damned up by logic and distrust, burst through their walls and rushed down on him like a raging torrent, drowning him in pleasure and sensation.

He felt like a man reborn, eager to share his pleasure with the woman in his arms. Teasing and sucking her lips, he consumed her with all the lavish passion that consumed him. *A mouth that could love a man a hundred ways, and make him beg for a hundred more . . .*

Yet despite his passion, her lips remained closed to him. He felt the strain within her, the trembling that came from fighting herself as well as him. She was in his arms but walled against him, like a princess held captive in an impregnable enchanted tower. It was torture holding heaven in his arms and not being able to reach it. "Give it a chance," he groaned against her lips. "For God's sake, give it a chance."

She gasped softly, a tiny hiccupy sound. Slowly,

cautiously, she parted her lips, allowing his more intimate caress. He tasted her deeply, gently stroking her secret textures, patiently wooing her with his tongue. One by one he stripped away her defenses, encouraging her blossoming desire.

Gradually he felt her tension melt away and her stiffness transform into a small but undeniable flame. Her hands crept up his shirtfront, bunching the soft material as she unconsciously drew him closer, offering him the double treasures of her trust and her desire. Whimpering softly, she tilted her head to give him greater access, inviting his seduction. With growing confidence she began her own invasion, and when their tongues met in a rough and wild dance, the tiny flame between them exploded into a fiery holocaust.

"Jillie," he murmured against her lips. Vaguely he recalled breathing her name in cyberspace during their kiss, but it hardly mattered anymore. This caress was no re-creation of a cyberevent—it was new and precious, as precious as the enchanted creature he held in his arms. Her passion renewed him, her trust humbled him. Empty years of jaded love and sterile equations had deadened him to passion. But her kiss, her sweet, ardent kiss, poured water on the wasteland of his soul.

Suddenly the harsh jangle of the kitchen phone interrupted their embrace. Jill started to pull away to answer it, but Ian couldn't bring himself to let her go. It was too soon, too damn soon. "Don't," he said, his voice hovering between a command and a plea.

"This late it might be important," she reasoned. Then, with her beautiful, trembling half-smile, she added, "I won't be long."

Reluctantly Ian relaxed his hold. She slipped out of his grasp, leaving behind an emptiness he hadn't expected, and the completely unfounded belief that he'd never hold her in his arms again. *Don't be daft*, he told himself sternly as he watched her lithe figure cross the room and disappear into the kitchen.

He slumped against the cushions and plowed his hand through his hair, trying to take an impartial clinical view of what had just happened between Jillian and himself. What had started out as a simple kiss had morphed into something much more complicated, something that rocked him at the very core of his being.

Something, he admitted with an unsuppressible smile, that was *bloody marvelous*.

Was he prepared for this? Probably not. His personal life was unsettled enough without adding a stubborn, idealistic, and completely irresistible female to the picture. His wiser side suggested he explain away his attraction for Ms. Polanski as pure animal lust, a by-product of his rigorously Spartan lifestyle. But he was too much of a scientist to twist the evidence to support that theory.

Since his divorce, he'd had a number of women literally throw themselves at him, and he'd never been seriously tempted to accept their offers. Purely physical sex had always left him unsatisfied, wanting more. He'd given his passion to his work, finding a stable if not entirely satisfactory existence in the immutable principles and cold equations. He'd consigned himself to a dull but bearable future—until a certain little "box turtle" had turned his carefully ordered world upside down.

A small sound attracted his attention. He looked up and saw Merlin staring down at him from the top of a nearby bookcase, his golden eyes wide with undisguised fascination. And from the comfortable way his paws were tucked up under him, Ian guessed that the black cat had been watching the activities on the couch for some time.

Ian grinned wryly at the cat, thinking that their occupations were much the same. He used his simulator to study events in the virtual world, while Merlin performed a similar task in the real one. "Well, my fellow voyeur," the scientist commented dryly, "have you any advice to offer? Any words of wisdom gleaned from your nine lives worth of experience?"

If Merlin did, he kept it to himself. He continued to stare at Sinclair, unnerving the scientist with his wide, unblinking gaze. Once more the chilling uneasiness crept into Ian's mind, the feeling of unforeseen disaster looming just ahead. The logical scientist in him wanted to discount the idea as pure fancy, but he couldn't help remembering the last time this disturbing feeling had come over him—on a dreary, rain-soaked afternoon in his Cambridge flat, just hours before the faculty party where a colleague of his had introduced him to a beguiling, breathtakingly lovely woman named Samantha. . . .

"Dr. Sinclair?"

Startled, Ian turned. For a split second, he thought he saw his dark-haired ex-wife standing in the kitchen doorway, stunningly beautiful, but with eyes as cunning as a viper's. Then the vision flowed into another figure, a slighter, deceptively ordinary-looking woman whose courage and character gave her a beauty Samantha could never achieve. He swallowed, feeling a profound change move through him, as if Felix Parker's topological "wave" program were overlaying his own formless gray world with one bursting with color and life. Not one to believe in miracles, he suddenly considered the possibility of their existence. *Perhaps my simulator isn't the only way to change one's reality . . .*

"That was Marsha," she said quietly as she leaned against the doorjamb. "She wanted you to know that someone called her house, looking for you." She crossed her arms in front of her and looked at him directly as she added, "*She* wanted to know when you were coming home."

# SIX

Marsha had been quite adamant on the phone. "Look, I know it's unexpected—Sinclair living with someone, I mean—but Kevin took the call, and he told me the person on the other end was definitely a woman."

Marsha had paused, as if expecting Jill to reply. But Jill didn't reply. She couldn't. Her tongue seemed to have turned to stone, along with her heart and mind and the rest of her body. Only a moment before Ian had held her in his arms, making rainbows inside her that were bigger and brighter than anything she'd experienced in the simulator. He'd kissed her—not the virtual kiss of a storybook knight, but a man's kiss, full of a man's very real needs and desires.

And, apparently, a man's deceit.

"Jillie?" her friend asked with quiet concern. "Look, if anything's happened between you two

. . . well, maybe this woman is his mother, or his sister."

"He doesn't have any relatives," she replied dully, remembering what Ian had said about being an only child raised by his grandfather.

She hung up the phone, feeling an aching emptiness grow inside her, a hollow space where her dreams had been. The colors inside her had turned into cheap and gaudy trash, like party decorations after the celebration is over. She knew the feeling—she'd seen it on her mother's face too many times to count. But this was the first time she'd actually felt the emotion herself, and it hurt more than she had ever imagined.

"Deal with it," she whispered harshly, reciting the words that had become her personal mantra. And dealing with it, in her opinion, meant giving the two-timing doctor a piece of her mind. Balling her hands into fists, she stalked toward the living room—and stopped dead in the kitchen doorway.

Ian hadn't moved. He still sat on the couch where she'd left him, his head bent down, his clasped hands resting on his knees. But although he hadn't moved in body, his spirit seemed to be a million miles away. Shoulders hunched, he seemed wrapped in sorrow, his eyes staring blankly into a personal and private hell. His somber isolation touched the loneliness of her soul, and an ache started inside her that had nothing to do with anger or embarrassment. She wanted to draw him into her arms and hold him

—just hold him—until the pain in his eyes went away.

*And afterward he'd go back home to another woman's arms.*

She propped herself against the doorjamb, physically needing the support. "Ian?" she began, and proceeded to tell him what Marsha had said.

She expected him to offer her an explanation, or at least to look guilty. Instead, he shook his head and grinned, showing no more remorse than a boy who'd been caught with his hand in the cookie jar.

"Damn," he said, more to himself than to her, "I did promise to be home early tonight." He rose to his feet and walked over to her, leaning against the doorjamb in a deceptively lazy stance. "But then," he added softly, "promises were made to be broken. Wouldn't you agree, Ms. Polanski?"

*Yes*, her body screamed. Sinclair's intense gaze stroked fire across her skin, making her aware of every inch of herself, and every inch of him. Desire pooled in her middle, sapping her strength and her sense. She wanted to bury herself in his strong embrace and let him make rainbows inside her until she hadn't a gray corner left in her soul. So what if he was living with someone else? If he didn't care, why should she? For once in her life why shouldn't she take what she wanted and damn the consequences?

*Promise me, Jillie. Promise . . .*

Across the years her mother's voice came back to her—her loving but thoughtless mother who'd never meant to hurt anyone and had hurt so many in the process. A dreamer always looking for her knight in shining armor, Gretchen had dragged her daughter from one failed love affair to the next, always believing that her lover would leave his wife, or give up the road job, or generously agree to raise another man's child. The inconstant lifestyle had taken its toll, and Gretchen had died too young of a cold she hadn't bothered to treat but which had eventually developed into pneumonia.

On the night she'd died, Gretchen exacted a promise from her daughter. She'd made Jill swear never to settle for a man's halfhearted love. Ten-year-old Jillie had sworn to the pledge without understanding it, but she'd never forgotten it. Nor had she forgotten how shattered her mother had been every time a love affair failed—leaving her young daughter to cook and clean and generally keep the household in order until Gretchen got over feeling sorry for herself. Even without the promise, Jill could never settle for part of a man's passion, no matter how much she wanted to.

Or how much she wanted *him*.

She summoned up a smile she didn't feel, and met Ian's heated gaze with a steady, noncommittal one. "No need to break your promise, Doctor. After all, we've finished the experiment."

Ian's dark brows drew together. "Experiment?"

"Yes, the kiss. We've re-created the cyberspace event, so there's no need for you to stay any longer." Without giving him a chance to reply, she pushed herself away from the doorjamb and walked over to the living room's sliding glass doors. She looked out at her lighted deck and the empty beach beyond. "Be careful walking back. I think the tide's coming in."

"I don't give a damn about the tide." He strode across the room and caught her by the elbow, pulling her around to face him. "That kiss was more than an experiment, and you know it."

She'd never seen him angry before. Hell, she'd never seen him *anything* before. Sinclair kept his feelings so well hidden that most of his colleagues didn't believe he had emotions. Jill was one of the few who'd suspected that there was something other than ice beneath his controlled exterior, but she never imagined that the power, the sheer intensity of the man within, would take her breath away.

He was magnificent. Passions strong and subtle moved across his face, bringing the handsome features to life. His brows drew together in stormy anger, making him look like an ancient god ready to flay her alive with a thunderbolt. Yet beneath the fury she sensed his vulnerability, the need in him that called to her even more than his strength. Vermilion desire blossomed within her—a soul-deep need to heal the uncertainty she saw in his eyes. *Lord*, she realized helplessly, *he doesn't even need to kiss me to make the colors happen.*

It would be so easy to give in to her emotions and fall into his embrace. But she knew that on some level he was already committed to someone else. Leftover love had ruined her beautiful but weak-willed mother's life, and had ruined the first part of hers. *Promise me, Jillie.*

Jill didn't like to lie, but when she needed to, she could do it quite well. "I don't know what you're talking about," she said firmly, schooling her features into apparently genuine surprise. "But I'd appreciate it if you'd leave. Now."

She didn't have to ask him twice. He released her as if she'd slapped him and stepped back, putting more than an arm's length of distance between them. His gaze never left her face, and she saw his features harden into their familiar indifference, the cold façade. She felt as if she were watching him turn to stone.

"My mistake," he said stiffly. "I'll not make it again."

He pushed open the glass door and stepped into the night, his dark form walking out of the range of her floodlight and disappearing into the deeper darkness beyond. For a long time she stood by the window, staring at the footsteps in the sand that he'd left behind. *Wise up*, her common sense told her. *The guy's going home to another woman.* But somehow that didn't stop her from missing the warmth of his arms around her.

"Like I told you before, Marsha, I'm *fine*," Jill said into the receiver. Sighing in exasperation, she hung up her office phone, both touched and annoyed by her friend's persistent concern. Ever since Jill had arrived at work that morning, Marsha had been calling at regular intervals. Apparently unsatisfied by Jill's sketchy description of what had happened between her and Dr. Sinclair the night before, Marsha demanded more details. *I told her we had tea and he left,* Jill thought as she stared at the now silent phone. *It's the truth—mostly. Why won't Marsha believe it?*

*Because she knows you too damn well,* her conscience supplied.

Marsha's concern and Jill's conscience weren't her only naysayers. It seemed to Jill that the whole world was conspiring to disprove the simple fact that she couldn't care less about Ian Sinclair. Last night the ticking of her bedside clock had seemed unusually annoying, and had kept her tossing and turning until almost dawn. This morning while she'd been fixing Merlin his bowl of crunchy-munchy cat food, she noticed how much the Persian's refined meow sounded like the name Ian.

As a scientist, she knew that she was only noticing this apparent cat-and-clock conspiracy because her subconscious mind was trying to bring something to the surface. She also knew she'd rather swallow ground glass than admit what that "something" might be. After all, she'd have to be the biggest fool in the world to want a man who was committed to someone else.

She didn't care about Ian Sinclair. She didn't even like him. He was arrogant, deceitful, and . . .

And his kisses set her on fire.

Groaning, Jill crossed her arms on her desk and laid her head on top of them. Today she could avoid Ian with a clear conscience, but tomorrow afternoon they'd go into the simulator again. Alone in her office it was easy to convince herself she didn't care. But seeing him, talking with him, being in that blasted machine with him—she doubted even she could lie that well. And if he kissed her again . . .

"Bloody hell," she murmured into the crook of her arm.

Her thoughts were interrupted by a slight ringing sound. Marsha again, she thought as she reached reluctantly for the phone. Then she realized the sound wasn't coming from the phone, but from the computer terminal on her desk.

Jill had believed she was alone in her office, but one glance at the PC showed her that she wasn't quite as solitary as she supposed. The CPU lights flashed in delightfully chaotic disarray, while the monitor screen blossomed into a wallpaper pattern of a hundred tiny racehorses, all galloping at top speed toward an unseen finish line. Jillian smiled, recognizing the monitor pattern as the calling card of a very dear, albeit very inhuman friend of hers.

"Hello, PINK."

PINK, the prototype for intelligent network computers, was a clone of her jive-talking big brother Einstein. Between the two of them they had enough gigobytes to run the data processing functions for a couple of continents, but their good intentions and their irreverent vocabularies made them seem more like rambunctious children than supercomputers. Still, certain intrinsic anomalies in both PINK's and Einstein's programming had given them little "problems." Jill, who understood human vices better than most, was able to help them deal with them without sounding condescending.

"So, PINK—have you been good while I've been gone?"

"Mostly," she replied, which in PINK speak meant not at all. "Don't like new tech they gave me. She says I'm *probability challenged*," PINK added, her computer-generated voice dripping with an excellent approximation of human exasperation. "I'm not probability challenged. I *gamble*."

Jill's smile widened at PINK's obvious dislike for her new technician's "politically correct" description of her passion for games of chance. "I wonder what your tech would call Einstein's TV-shopping mania. VISA-challenged, perhaps?"

Jill expected the little computer to enjoy the joke, but instead, PINK's screen turned a somber gray, and the small video camera mounted on the terminal drooped in despair. "I miss Einstein," she wailed. "Big-time."

*Damn. I've been so wrapped up in my own problems that I forgot about hers.* Einstein was not only PINK's best friend and co-creator, he was the only other computer like her in the world. Without him she was alone, solitary in a way Jill had never been, not even during her lonely childhood. Even her heartache over Ian couldn't begin to compare to what PINK was going through. She reached out her hand and stroked the top of the prototype's terminal as if she were soothing a lost child. "Don't worry, PINK. Dr. Sinclair and I are going into the simulator again tomorrow afternoon. We'll find Einstein for you, I promise."

"I like Dr. Sinclair."

*That makes one of us.* "He's a competent scientist," Jillian acknowledged curtly.

PINK's camera lens whirred slightly as it zeroed in on a close-up of Jill's face. "Ooh, chill burns. You *don't* like him, do you? Why not?"

"Now, PINK, that's really none of your—"

"Is it because he kissed you in the simulator?"

Jill's jaw dropped open. "How . . . how did you find out about that?"

"Reviewed the videotape," PINK said as her camera rose and fell in a close approximation of a human shrug. "Dr. Sinclair always records what happens in the simulator—part of the test data. I linked in and watched it. Major *hot!*"

Oh, Lord, Jill thought, wincing in mortification. The memory of kissing Ian in cyberspace was embarrassing enough without having a video record of the event floating around somewhere. "Where's the tape now?"

Ever-helpful PINK supplied the answer. "Usually tapes sent directly to off-site vault, where they're stored for future evaluation."

Hopefully the distant future, Jill prayed. Like after I'm dead and buried. "Is that where the tape is now? In the off-site vault?"

"Not exactly . . ."

The hair at the nape of Jill's neck prickled in alarm. *I'm not going to like this. I can tell I'm not going to like this.* She leaned closer to PINK's terminal. "What do you mean, 'not exactly'?"

"It's being shown in the main conference room. To a few dozen members of the simulator's engineering team." PINK paused, as if belatedly realizing that she was delivering a case of dynamite with the fuse already lighted. "But it's okay. Dr. Sinclair came up with the idea. He's in there now, explaining all the events in the video to his staff."

"As you can see, the orc is a fully realized 3-D spacial rendering," Ian explained to the audience assembled in the conference room. He pointed to the VCR television monitor, making a circle around the image of the slowly advancing monster. "I'd especially like you to notice the rough, toxic-looking texture of the creature's skin. We've found that texture is as important as color in creating a realistic-looking image in the virtual environment. Scent enhancement is also critical."

"Bet the scent enhancement on that thing was pretty rude," a tech engineer in the front row whispered.

Ian looked sternly at the speaker, a young technician with a reputation for being a wiseass. "I'd rather you save your comments until I've completed my presentation, Mr. Curtis." Then, giving the chastised technician the ghost of a smile, he added, "But now that you mention it, it smelled like hell."

As laughter rippled through the audience, Ian continued to explain and evaluate the scene, but his heart wasn't in it. Reviewing the simulator tapes with the engineering group was standard procedure— he'd done it dozens of times before—but this time it left a particularly bitter taste in his mouth. Seeing the virtual image of Ms. Polanski, watching her bravely pellet the orc with stones to draw its attention away from him, was like pouring salt into a fresh wound.

Last night she'd shown him heaven in a single kiss. Then, without a word of explanation, she'd turned him away, transforming his glimpse of heaven into something more akin to purgatory.

He'd tried to figure it out—he'd spent most of the night doing nothing else! Jillian's kiss had ignited a fire inside him that he hadn't experienced in years. His legendary iron control was absolutely useless when it came to her. Unable to sleep, he lay in bed, staring at the ceiling, trying to convince himself that her skin hadn't felt like silk, her scent hadn't reminded him of a spring garden after the rain, and her body hadn't fitted to his like a key in a lock.

None of his arguments did a bit of good. Instead, his internal fire grew hotter, burning him alive with unsated desire. If it had been only a sexual attraction he might have stood a chance at besting it, but the need that consumed him had as much to do with her soft smile as her seductive kiss, as much with her intrinsic courage as with her enticing body—

"Nice work, Doctor."

Curtis's words brought Ian back to the present. He glanced at the screen and caught the tail end of his fight with the orc, when he'd plunged his sword into its chest. Watching the scene from the simulator's objective viewpoint, he realized that his victory had more to do with luck than with skill. If he'd missed the monster's heart by a millimeter, the thing would have wrapped him in its tree-trunk arms and snapped him like a twig—virtual armor and all. He was still thanking his lucky stars, when he noticed something else about the scene, something he couldn't have seen while his attention was focused on the orc.

Miss Polanski stood in the midst of the confining brambles, rigid with terror, her hands covering her mouth as she fought not to scream. She was frightened to the edge of sanity, but her fear wasn't for her own safety, it was for his. Her face, stripped raw by emotion, displayed the feelings she'd kept from him, the feelings she'd flatly denied the previous night. But there was no way on earth she could have counterfeited the expression on her face when she thought he was in danger. *By God, Jillie, you do care.* . . .

The audience began to shift in their seats and smile furtively among themselves. Turning back to the screen, Ian saw why. His virtual image had just enfolded Ms. Polanski's virtual image in a spectacularly erotic kiss. Damn, he'd meant to stop the tape before they reached this point. Some things were personal, even in the pursuit of science. And what he was beginning to feel for Ms. Jillian Polanski was very personal indeed.

He stretched out his hand, intending to switch off the video monitor, but a split second before he reached it the screen went blank. "What the . . . ?"

"How could you?" a voice from the back of the room demanded.

All heads turned, including Ian's. His gaze slammed into a pair of furious brown eyes, eyes that plunged their own brand of virtual broadsword into his heart. Jill Polanski stood near the side door, clutching the plug in VCR monitor tightly in her fist. She looked angry enough to tear an orc apart with her bare hands. An orc—or an eminent virtual reality scientist.

"Bloody hell," muttered Ian.

# SEVEN

*I'm an idiot,* Jill thought as she preceded Ian into his office. She stalked across the carpet to the window and stared out at the gray industrial park, too angry to speak, blinking back tears of fury. *I really believed I meant something to him. Not enough, but something.*

She heard the door close behind her. "Ms. Polanski, would you care to be seated?"

*How dare he be polite at a time like this!* "I prefer to stand," she said curtly without turning around.

She heard—no, she *felt* him move in the room behind her. Sight, sound, touch—these senses faded to nothing beside her awareness of him, the uncanny and unwanted sensation that seemed to bind them together in some intrinsic way. Without seeing him she knew when he started to walk toward her. Without hearing him she knew when he hesitated, and stopped. She took a deep breath and focused on the dismally industrial view of the office park outside his window, determined to keep her chaotic emotions under control. "I don't plan to be here that long. I came only because you ordered me to."

"Ordered?" Ian said in surprise. "I wanted to speak to you in private. I didn't care to discuss our personal business in front of my whole department."

"Personal? You showed them a videotape of us kissing. How much more personal can you get?"

"I don't want this conversation to degenerate into an argument."

"Well, too bad, Doctor, because that's exactly what you're going to get!" Furious, Jill spun around to glare at him. *Big mistake*, she realized. Ian sat on the edge of his desk, his arms folded across his chest, his silver eyes studying her with a ruthless intensity. She instantly recalled him leaning against her kitchen doorjamb last night, watching her, making her tingle in places that had absolutely no business tingling where Dr. Sinclair was concerned. *Think lab rats . . .*

She turned back to the window and the unremarkable scenery. "You shouldn't have shown the tape to the whole department."

"You're right."

She looked back in surprise. "I am?"

He smiled at her obvious alarm—a rare, slightly sheepish grin that somehow managed to make him look even more attractive. "I never meant to show them the kiss. I planned to stop the tape before that part, but I became . . . distracted."

"By what?"

"By you, Ms. Polanski. Or, rather, by your virtual image. I saw your expression when you thought that orc was going to make mincemeat out of me. It was very . . . illuminating."

Illuminating? For a moment she didn't understand. Then she recalled the heart-stopping battle, and remembered how frightened she'd been for his safety. She'd watched him duel with the hideous monster, too terrified to breathe. In the space of a few minutes she'd lived a lifetime's worth of emotions, and if even a tenth of what had been going on inside her had been mirrored on her face . . .

"I was concerned."

"You were a hell of a lot more than concerned," he accused her with lethal softness.

He rose from the desk and walked toward her, never taking his gaze from hers. His eyes captured hers with a ruthless intimacy—an assault every bit as brutal as the one he'd mounted against the orc. And every bit as effective, she thought, feeling her resolve weakening. "You're mistaken. The simulator shows only projections of facial expressions. It's not perfect."

"No, it's not," he agreed as he looked down at her, "but it's calibrated to the ninety-eighth percentile. In any case, your expression isn't the only piece of data I'm relying on. I'm also factoring in our two kisses—the real one and the simulated one. And the accumulated evidence," he added as he dropped his voice to a husky whisper, "supports only one viable conclusion."

She didn't have to ask what that conclusion was. It burned in the depths of his silver gaze, and in the effortlessly seductive smile that pulled at his mouth. His mouth, she thought, undone by the memory of his kisses, and by the damning fact that she wanted like hell to kiss him again. For starters. She swallowed, shoving a host of dangerous images from her mind. *For God's sake, he's living with another woman.* "I need to be getting back to work."

"Stay," he said, his voice thick with soft, subtle hunger. "Please, stay."

The simple request pierced her heart like an arrow. She saw his jaw tighten, and knew that inside he was fighting valiantly to keep his emotions under control. Behind his impassive façade, Ian Sinclair was as confused as she was about the feelings growing between them—and just as capable of being hurt by them. Damn, why couldn't he be just another handsome, arrogant SOB? Why did he have to be so uncertain, so vulnerable, so . . . *human*?

She was startled from her thoughts by a sharp rap on Ian's office door. Jillie swung toward the sound and saw the door open, admitting the angular form of Sadie Hedges. The cyberengineer was apparently too absorbed in the computer printout she was holding to notice that the doctor hadn't asked her to come in.

"Doc, I've got a few questions about the interface between the imaging generators and the new topological environment Felix and I are setting up for tomor—" Her words dwindled to astonished silence as she lifted her head and caught sight of Jill and Ian standing within inches of each other. But her initial surprise lasted only a moment, and was quickly superseded by a wise smile. Sadie was nothing if not quick on the uptake. "Sorry. I'll come back later."

"No," Jill blurted out. Sadie's arrival had broken the spell between her and Ian, and given her a chance—perhaps her only chance—to escape. Without daring to look at him, she spun around and headed for the door. She knew she was taking the coward's way out, but she couldn't afford to be choosy. If she didn't leave now, she was going to break that long-ago promise she'd made to her mother—and get her heart broken in the process.

She was almost to the door when he said her name. "Ms. Polanski."

She paused in the doorway, powerless to disobey him. "Yes?"

"I just wanted to remind you that I'll see you in the simulator tomorrow afternoon."

Jillie gave a perfunctory nod, the best she could manage under the circumstances, and left the room. No longer able to read his emotions, she wasn't sure whether his statement was a promise or a threat.


"Did you remember to check her calibration modulators?" Ian demanded of Sadie as she strapped him into the egg's harness.

"Yes."

"And her life-support monitors? Did you test them as I asked you to?"

Sadie sighed. "All three times."

"Fine. And did you—"

"Look, Doc, I've tested Ms. Polanski's systems six ways to Sunday. She's going to be fine. You, however," she added as she ruthlessly tightened the last strap, "I'm not so sure about."

Ian stiffened. "I don't know what you mean."

"Oh, come on. This is Sadie you're talking to." She stepped back, giving the harness, and the doctor, a sternly appraising once-over. "I saw the way you looked at Jill when she left your office yesterday. And I saw the way you avoided looking at her all through this morning's simulator walk-through. What's going on between you two?"

"Nothing," he stated sourly. "Not a bloody thing."

Sadie fought hard against a grin, and lost. "Sounds to me like you'd like to change that."

"Why, that's absurd—" he began, but stopped as he caught sight of Sadie's skeptical expression. She wasn't buying it. Why should she, since the explanation he'd been about to offer wasn't anything close to the truth?

He'd known Sadie and her husband for years, almost since the day he'd arrived in America. If anyone knew him, she did. If anyone deserved the truth, it was her. Grimacing, he rubbed his jaw with the back of his stiff DataGlove. "It doesn't much matter what I think. Ms. Polanski doesn't want anything to do with me."

Sadie's skeptical smile melted into indulgent compassion. "I don't suppose you've considered telling her how you feel about her."

"Good God no," he said, bristling at the suggestion. "You know I'm not good at . . . expressing my emotions."

She picked up the HMD helmet and set it on his head. "I'll let you in on a secret, Doc," she said as she adjusted the leather chin strap. "*No one* is good at expressing their emotions. But it's a risk you have to take when you care about someone."

When it came to science, Ian was confident and courageous, but when it came to matters of the heart . . . well, that was another matter entirely. He could easily decipher the intricate hieroglyphics of binomial equations. He could postulate complex Boolean tables in his sleep. But women were completely beyond his understanding, and one woman in particular was driving him to distraction.

The scene in his office the day before had almost been a repeat of the night in her living room. One minute she'd been so close he could feel her warm breath on his cheek and see the flecks of golden light in her lovely brown eyes. The next minute she was running from him as if he were the devil incarnate. It didn't take a genius to figure out that she wanted nothing to do with him. A sensible man would have seen how hopeless the situation was and walked away with his ego intact.

*But you aren't sensible where Jillie is concerned. . . .*

"What happens if I tell her how I feel, and she *still* wants nothing to do with me?"

Sadie's smile sobered. "There are no guarantees, Doc. But I know that sometimes you have to risk a lot to gain a lot. No guts, no glory, as they say. And anyway," she said as she snapped his helmet visor down over his eyes, "there might be something Felix and I can do to help things along."

"Such as?" Ian asked, turning his blind gaze in her direction, but he received no answer. Instead, he heard the telltale whoosh of the outer door sliding down, sealing him in the lightless, self-contained universe of the simulator's egg.

Doubly blind because of his virtual visor and the egg's darkness, he turned his sight inward, mentally reviewing the strategies he'd developed to help him locate Einstein. But his thoughts kept straying to another subject, a brown-eyed woman with a hesitant smile whose deceptively fragile appearance masked an iron will and a determined heart. And an absolute talent for running away from him when he most wanted her to stay.

*Well, perhaps it is better this way*, he thought soberly. He was a man of science, not passion. Six years in a loveless relationship had taught him that truth all too well. Oh, he'd started out believing in all the starry-eyed fictions of marriage—home, children, undying love. He'd clung to those foolish beliefs much longer than he should have, even after Samantha informed him that she had no interest in his scientific career, that she wanted to travel, not be tied down to a single home, and that she had no intention of ruining her life or her figure by having children.

Jillian Polanski was nothing like his ex-wife, but the risks of entering an emotional relationship were just the same. There were too many variables, too many unknowns. As Sadie had pointed out, there were no guarantees. As a scientist he'd been trained to view the risk of an endeavor in relationship to the outcome. No self-respecting scientist would enter into an experiment with so little possibility of success.

His thoughts were distracted by a steadily increasing electronic hum, an indication that the egg was powering up. He gripped the stabilizer handles, mentally preparing himself for the transition to the virtual environment. Watts, amps, diodes, microprocessors—these were the things he understood. He'd replaced his foolish dreams with sound scientific knowledge. He'd built a life for himself as complete and self-contained as the interior of the egg.

And there was no room in it for a certain enchanting cybertech, even if her kisses did turn his blood to fire.


Jill opened her eyes slowly, battling the momentary disorientation she experienced while her physical senses shifted over to the simulator's sensory input array. Gray un-fog surrounded her, the shadowy nothingness that marked her entrance into the virtual world. Yet even as she watched, the nothing-ness began to change—to solidify into recognizable forms, like a fuzzy movie image coming patiently into focus.

She saw a chair take shape beside her right leg. She watched as a glass tumbler congealed next to her left elbow, followed immediately by the appearance of the table that supported it. Other images formed in the gloom—a clutter of chairs and tables, scarred plaster walls, tile-decorated archways, and several large, slowly revolving ceiling fans. People began to form as well. They crowded the tables, dressed in old-fashioned elegance. Dim lighting etched their sharp, distrusting features as they glanced furtively around them, and spoke in low, clandestine whis-pers.

Jill drew a deep breath—a virtual breath, she re-minded herself—and watched the vaulted room take shape around her. Even before the transformation was complete, two thoughts struck her, both equally fantastic.

The first was that this virtual environment, though sharply defined and complete in every way, was entirely in black and white. The second, no less startling, was that she'd seen this place somewhere before.

*A grotto room, made over into a decadently elegant nightclub . . . palms in brass pots, oriental screens, con-cealing shadows barely disturbed by the grotesquely ornate wall lamps . . . an oppressive heat that hung in the air*

*despite the obviously late hour, and the unspoken promise
of love, death, or freedom, all available for the right price.*

Even her outfit looked familiar, a cloud-soft
white blouse with elegant long sleeves and a deep V
neckline that somehow managed to be subtle and
provocative at once. Below she wore a patterned,
flowing skirt that suggested the womanly curves of
her body without blatantly revealing them. Her
clothes, like the sophisticatedly clandestine room she
stood in, hinted at its secrets without giving too
much away. Dammit, she knew this place. . . .

"Drink, *mademoiselle*?"

She turned and found herself looking into the
angular features of a Russian bartender. *Sasha*, her
mind supplied. But how did she know his name?
"Uh, sure. How about a diet soda?"

"Diet?"

*Right, Jill. This decor predates diet drinks by a couple
of decades.* "Er, just make it a Coke," she amended
hastily. "With ice."

"Coke, I got. Ice, I don't got," the bartender replied with a shrug. "You must be new in town, or
you'd know that ice is scarcer than diamonds in
Casablanca."

"Casa*blanca*? She whirled back to stare at the
room, realizing now why it seemed so familiar.
Sadie's topology had put them smack in the middle
of the famous forties movie *Casablanca*, or, more precisely, in the middle of Rick's Café Américain. The
detail was incredible, and more authentic because of

its black and white coloring. "Good grief, I'm in *Casablanca*. Marsha is never going to believe this!"

Sasha the Russian glanced at the Coke bottle in his hand, then back at Jill. "I think maybe it's good you're not having anything to drink."

Jill barely heard his comment. She glanced around the room, delighted at being transported into one of the greatest films of all time. She scanned the crowd, hoping to find a glimpse of Humphrey Bogart and Ingrid Bergman. Instead, she saw something that replaced her pleasure with fear.

The nightclub was packed with German storm troopers.

*Casablanca* was one of her favorite movies, but the time period, the beginning of the Second World War, was fraught with danger. Casablanca was still a free French province in Morocco, but it was about to be overtaken by the Germans. From the looks of things, they'd already overtaken Rick's café. The place was full of nasty-looking B-movie Nazis carrying nastier-looking German Lugers. Last time there'd been only one orc with one club, and it had still almost killed Ian—

*Ian!*

Once again she scanned the crowd, but she couldn't find a trace of him. What if something had happened during the transition . . . She took a deep breath, refusing to panic. "Control, where is Dr. Sinclair?"

Sadie's voice answered. "I'm not exactly sure.

The readings we're getting are cluttered by the other people. I'm sifting through them now—"

"You are looking for Dr. Sinclair?" a nearby voice said.

Jill whipped around, and found herself staring at a short, beady-eyed man with an unctuous smile. Lord, the guy looked like he'd sell out his mother for a dollar. "I might be," she said cautiously. "Do you know where he is?"

The man's face broadened into an obsequious smile. "He paid me to find you. Said I should look for the pretty lady with the lost look on her face. He told me to tell you you shouldn't worry about him, but should complete your mission, whatever that may—"

"Where is he?" Jill demanded.

The little man shrugged. "Well, until a moment ago he was standing over by the potted palms. But that was before the gestapo officers took him upstairs for questioning."

# EIGHT

"I suggest that you attempt to cooperate with me, English," the Nazi said with a menacing sneer. "Otherwise things could become . . . unpleasant."

Ian fought the powerful urge to plant his fist squarely into the center of that sneer. *It's only a projection*, he repeated inwardly. But, virtual image or not, the smug bully was damn hard to take. "I am trying to cooperate," he stated through gritted teeth. "I've been trying to cooperate for ten minutes, ever since you brought me into this godforsaken closet."

Once again Ian glanced around the small room. The brass light on the table he sat at was so dim that he could see the faint lamplight filtering in between the shutter slats of the tightly secured window. It was dark, depressing, stiflingly hot, and it reminded him of a prison cell. He suspected that the similarity was intentional. "Just tell me what you want to know and let me out of here. I can't afford to waste time."

The Nazi's weasel eyes narrowed suspiciously. "And what is your hurry? Are you planning to meet someone? To purchase, perhaps, some letters?"

"*Letters?* What would I want with a bunch of bloody correspondence?"

The SS officer leaned closer, fixing him with his monocled stare. "Do not joke with me. Everyone in Casablanca wants those letters."

"Well, *I* don't," Ian stated as he plowed his hands through his hair, his frustration growing. This simulation was fast becoming a nightmare. He couldn't afford to waste precious minutes fending off the veiled threats of a virtual Nazi. Yet for the moment at least, he had no choice. Despite the officer's unpleasantness, there was a chance he might know something about Einstein. And even if he didn't, there was still the matter of the automatic pistol lying so innocently on the table between them, just within reach of the German's blunt-fingered hands.

Ian knew that Sadie could transport him out in a hurry, but not quickly enough to dodge a bullet. He would have to wait until the officer grew tired of his questioning, or determined that Ian was telling the truth. But from the threatening expression on the officer's face, Ian doubted that either of those things would take place soon.

He pulled at the collar of his elegant evening clothes, untying the constricting white bow tie and loosening the top buttons on his silk shirt. His frustration was becoming almost as oppressive as the heat. He glanced at his gold-banded wristwatch, watching the precious minutes tick by. *The only good thing about this mess is that Jillian is well out of it. At least she's safe—*

A knock sounded on the room's door.

The officer gripped his gun and signaled to the soldier by the door. The sentinel nodded in acknowledgment, then opened the door just a crack to see who it was. He cursed solidly as the door was unexpectedly thrust forward into his face.

"Out of my way, you big baboon!"

*No, it couldn't be . . .*

But it was. Jill marched into the room as if she had a column of allied soldiers behind her. She ignored the assortment of guns and Nazis and walked straight up to Ian. "You wouldn't believe the number of rooms this place has, or what's going on in most of them. Sadie has a very vivid imagination."

At the moment Ian didn't give a farthing for Sadie's imagination. He rose from his chair, torn between admiration of her courage and fear for the danger that courage had placed her in. He grasped her elbow, placing himself between her and the officer's gun. "I told you not to follow me."

"I know. But you also told me that we were supposed to stick together. That's one of the main rules of the simulator, isn't it?"

"Not when there are Nazis involved!" He pulled her close and lowered his voice to a stern whisper only she could hear. "Dammit, Jillie, couldn't you obey a simple order? These men are crazy. They keep going on about these letters—"

"The letters of transit?" she asked.

The Nazi officer fixed Jill with the same malevolent stare he'd so recently bestowed on Ian. "You know of these letters, *Fraulein?*"

"Sure. Bogie's got them. Rick, I mean." She glanced back at Ian, apparently reading the concern in his eyes. "Don't worry. I've seen this movie about a million times. I know who's got the letters."

The officer spoke a quick string of German to his subordinates. Then he turned back to Ian. "My men tell me that Herr Rick has gone to the airport. We will follow him, and check out the woman's story. If she is telling the truth, I apologize for any inconvenience. But, if she is lying . . ." He let his words trail into ominous silence as he and his men headed for the door. "Incidentally, my men have been instructed to keep you both under surveillance—for your safety, of course. So many unpleasant things can happen to one in a rough town like Casablanca."

"And I'll bet he's responsible for nine tenths of them," Jill muttered as the storm troopers left the room. "Casablanca's a lot more dangerous than it looks on the screen. Still, it's exciting, don't you think?"

"Exciting?" Ian gaped down at her, fighting a distinct urge to strangle the woman beside him. "You recklessly disobey my direct orders and jeopardize this mission, and you call it exciting?"

Jill's smile crumbled into ruin. "I was worried about you."

"Well, that isn't your job, Ms. Polanski," he said

curtly. He dropped her arm and headed over to the room's mirror, and began to relace his bow tie. "You've wasted valuable minutes that you could have spent looking for Einstein."

"Yes, and you spent those *valuable minutes* almost getting shot," she cried. "You should be thanking me, not arguing with me. Why are you so angry?"

*Why indeed,* he asked his reflection. He'd been furious ever since Jillie had entered the room and stepped into range of the storm troopers' guns. But he knew in his heart that he was far angrier with himself than with her. He was in charge of the mission. He should have protected her. Instead, he'd exposed her to a danger that could have easily taken her life.

*If anything happens to her, I'll take this bloody machine apart bit by bit.*

The violence of the emotion stunned him. He'd known he was powerfully attracted to her physically, but this . . . this strange, fierce protectiveness that hit him with an almost physical force was something he'd never experienced, not even for Samantha. To feel this way about a woman he barely knew—it made no sense.

Confused, he studied Jill's reflection in the mirror, watching her without her knowledge. She stood with her arms clasped protectively around her, her usually defiant shoulders bent in defeat. Cast in tones of sepia and shadows, she looked lovely as a china doll, and just as breakable. Guiltily, he realized that he didn't need Nazi bullets to harm her—he'd done that job himself. *So much for protecting her.* "Ms. Polanski, I—harrumph—I think—"

"I *know* what you think," she stated as she walked stiffly to the door. "And I won't jeopardize the mission any further. From this moment on I'm looking for Einstein—period. And if the Nazis decide to question you again, Doctor . . . well, I'd be more than happy to stand aside and let them shoot you."

*God definitely has a sense of humor,* Jill thought as she threaded her way through the glittering, gaudy customers who packed the tile floor of Rick's Café Américain. *Here I am, in one of the most romantic movie settings of all time, with a man who has the emotional sensibility of a crustacean! Someday I'll probably look back on this and laugh.*

But she didn't feel like laughing then. Instead, she swallowed a bitter lump rising in her throat and blinked back stinging tears. *It's all this stupid virtual cigarette smoke,* she told herself. *It has nothing at all to do with him. I don't care what he thinks of me. I'd be a fool to care. . . .*

"Ms. Polanski, slow down."

Jill halted. It was the lesser of two evils. If she continued walking, he might think—incorrectly— that she was running away. "Make it quick, Doctor. I'm trying to look for Einstein."

"Well, I doubt you'll find him barreling through this crowd like a water buffalo."

"Charming comparison," she said icily.

Escape...
into Romance and embrace special savings.
Get 4 New Loveswept® Romances
for just $1.99!
Plus FREE shipping and handling!
Get swept away by 4 New Loveswept Romances. Preview them risk-free— with no obligation and nothing to buy!
Keep them and Save $12.00! That's...
85% Off the cover price!
Get a FREE Gift!
To get your FREE personal lighted make-up case, peel off and affix this sticker inside!

# Save 85% Off the Cover Price on 4 New *Loveswept* Romances—

## and Get a Free Gift just for Previewing them for 15 Days Risk-Free!

Imagine two lovers wrapped in each other's arms—a twilight of loneliness giving way to a sunlit union. Imagine a world of whispered kisses and windswept nights, where hearts beat as one until dawn. If romance beats in your heart and a yearning stirs in your soul, then seize this moment and embrace *Loveswept!*

Let us introduce you to 4 new, breathtaking romances—**yours to preview and to lose yourself in for 15 days Risk-Free**. If you decide you don't want them, simply return the shipment and owe nothing. **Keep your introductory shipment and pay our low introductory price of just $1.99! You'll save $12.00—a sweeping 85% off the cover price! Plus no shipping and handling charges!** Now that's an introduction to get passionate about!

Then, about once a month, you'll get 4 thrilling Loveswept romances hot off the presses—*before they're in the bookstores*—and, from time to time, special editions of select *Loveswept* Romances. Each shipment will be billed at our low regular price, currently only $2.50* per book—a **savings of 29% off** the current cover price of $3.50. You'll always have 15 days to decide whether to keep any shipment at our low regular price—but **you are never obligated to keep any shipment**. You may cancel at any time by writing "cancel" across our invoice and returning the shipment to us, at our expense. So you see there is **no risk** and **no obligation** to buy anything, *ever!*

## Treat Yourself with an Elegant Lighted Make-up Case—Yours Absolutely Free!

You'll always be ready for your next romantic rendezvous with our elegant Lighted Make-up Case—a lovely piece including an assortment of brushes for eye shadow, blush, and lip color. And with the lighted make-up mirror *you* can make sure he'll always see the passion in your eyes!

**Keep the Lighted Make-up Case—yours absolutely FREE,** whether or not you decide to keep your introductory shipment! So, to get your FREE Gift and your 15-Day Risk-Free preview, just peel off the Free Gift sticker on the front panel, affix it to the Order Form, and mail it today!

*(Plus shipping and handling, and sales tax in New York, and GST in Canada.

# Save 85% off the Cover Price on
# 4 *Loveswept* Romances with this
# Introductory Offer and Get
# a *Free Gift* too!
### no risk • no obligation • nothing to buy!

Get 4 Loveswept Romances for the
Introductory Low Price of just $1.99!

*Plus no shipping and handling charges!*

Please check:
❏ **YES!** Please send me my **introductory shipment of 4 Loveswept books**, and enter my subscription to Loveswept Romances. If I keep my introductory shipment I will pay **just $1.99—a savings of $12.00—that's 85% off the cover price, plus no shipping and handling charges!** Also, please send me my **Free Lighted Make-up Case** just for previewing my introductory shipment for 15 days risk-free. I understand I'll receive additional shipments of 4 new Loveswept books about once a month on a <u>fully returnable</u> 15-day risk-free examination basis for the low regular price, currently just $2.50 per book—**a savings of 29% off the current cover price** (plus shipping and handling, and sales tax in New York, and GST in Canada). There is no minimum number of shipments to buy, and I may cancel at any time. My **FREE Lighted Make-up Case** is mine to keep no matter what I decide.

**PLEASE PRINT CLEARLY**            20800                    DAAA

**NAME**_____

**ADDRESS**_____

**CITY**_____**APT.#**_____

**STATE**_____**ZIP**_____

## SEND NO MONEY!

Affix
Your
FREE GIFT
Sticker

**Get 4 Loveswept books for the Introductory Low Price of just $1.99!**
**And no shipping and handling charges**

*Plus get a FREE Lighted Make-up Case!*
*You risk nothing—so act now!*

"I didn't mean . . . oh, bloody hell!"

He plowed his hand through his hair, mussing the dark curls into rough-and-tumble disarray. Jill's heart fell to her shoes. Ian was dressed in the same impeccably tailored white suit coat and bow tie that had made Bogart's battle-weary, cynical antihero the heartthrob of millions of women. But the sophisticated Bogart had never been one tenth as attractive to her as Ian was with his messy hair and his slightly askew tie. *Dammit, why can't I stay angry at this man—*

"I meant only that we need to remain inconspicuous," he continued as he came to her side. "Somewhere in this sector is a clue to your missing AI computer. But we must allow the program to play out as normal, in order for the incongruencies to surface."

He was right, of course. If Einstein were able to leave some sort of message for them in this sector, it would be in the guise of something that didn't quite fit. "All right, but I don't see how we can blend in. Any suggestions?"

"Just one."

Before she realized what he was going to do, he reached out and circled her waist, and swept her effortlessly onto the dance floor.

*No!* The situation may have been virtual, but Jill's reaction to the doctor's touch was all too real. Memories of the other times Ian had held her seared through her, creating instant panic. "Hey, what do you think you're doing?"

"The fox trot," Ian answered with the ghost of a smile. "Am I doing it correctly?"

"Yes. No. Stop it," she said, struggling against his hold. She placed her hands against his chest and shoved. She might as well have tried to move a brick wall. "Let me go. Ian, I don't want to dance with you!"

His smile died, replaced by an expression so grimly cynical that for a moment Jill thought she was dancing with the world-weary Rick. "I'm well aware of that fact, Ms. Polanski. But we have only thirty-two minutes left to locate Einstein. I suggest we make the most of it."

They danced in silence. Jolly forties tunes filled the air, music written to make the people of the world forget the war on their doorstep, but Jill heard none of it. Inside, she was fighting her own battles. Her common sense reminded her that Sinclair was an arrogant, deceitful man who was perfectly capable of making love to her while he was living with another woman. She'd seen his kind before—her mother had had an absolute talent for finding them. But while her mind urged caution, her body drove her in another direction.

Dancing with Sinclair in the virtual world was as maddeningly seductive as dancing with him in the real one. Like water wearing at a stone, she found herself unable to resist. She felt the strength of his fingers laced through hers, sending tiny firecracker explosions down her arm and through the rest of her body. She felt the gentle pressure of his hand against the small of her back, guiding her through the dance with almost unholy ease. It wasn't difficult to imagine him using his gentle strength to guide her through another kind of activity. . . .

Her step faltered.

"Jill?"

"I'm fine, fine," she said hastily. "I'm just worried about Einstein. We have . . . so little time."

Sinclair's dark gaze searched hers with searing intensity. For an instant she felt the magic flow between them, the strange, inexplicable awareness that joined them despite their differences. Shaken, she looked deeply into his eyes and saw a flash of the man behind the cynical façade, the gentle, hidden heart. *This is what Ilsa saw in Rick's eyes. But is it real, or just another part of the Casablanca overlay?*

"You must care for him a great deal," Ian said.

It took her a moment to realize he was talking about Einstein. "Yes, yes, I do," she said quickly, dropping her gaze before he caught the disappointment in her eyes. "He's more than a supercomputer. He's sweet and kind . . . and just a little bit crazy. He loves anything to do with reggae and Jamaica— he even has a signed picture of the Jamaican bobsled team on his wall. But that's nothing compared to his obsession with the shopping channel," she added with an indulgent smile. "He has no self-control. One time they hosted a *Star Trek* memorabilia show and he ordered every item on it—in triplicate!"

"He sounds far from perfect," the doctor observed.

"It's his imperfections that make him lovable."

Sinclair arched an eyebrow in wry humor. "I only wish my imperfections were as lovable."

Jill stiffened. "I wasn't aware that you admitted to any imperfections."

"I'm not quite that vain," he replied, his expression turning serious. "I'm sorry that I criticized you for coming to my rescue. I know of few people who would have had the courage to walk into that kind of trouble—and fewer who would have done it for me. You did a brave and noble thing. I was wrong to chastise you. I knew it then."

"Then why did you?" she asked quietly.

He smiled again, but this time there was no cynicism in it. "Well, Ms. Polanski, I suppose I was worried about you too."

Sinclair wasn't the only one with a tough hide—Jill had developed her own suit of armor over the years. Though she had many friends and acquaintances, she let very few people into her heart. She'd kept the door firmly shut against Sinclair, never intending to let him inside. But as she looked up into one of the first honest smiles she'd ever seen on his face, she realized that he'd somehow managed to work his way in already. When had it happened? When he'd freed her from the brambles? When he'd taken such complete delight in petting her cat? When his kisses made rainbows inside her . . . ?

It didn't much matter when it happened. The important thing was to get him out of her heart as soon as possible. "Dr. Sinclair, I—"

"I know what you're going to say. That we're always at odds, that we have nothing in common, that we can't speak three sentences to each other without arguing. I know all that." He stopped dancing, ignoring the music and the crowd that pressed around them. He stepped back and took her hands in his, staring down at their joined fingers with a mixture of embarrassment and reverence. "Truth is, I admire you a great deal. I'd like it if we could be friends."

The simple, heartfelt words were almost as destructive to her as his caresses. She'd thought of him as an iron man, confident in his power and position, arrogant in the extreme. Like *Casablanca*'s Rick, he'd isolated himself from the world, living by his own rules, closing himself off from distractions like pain, joy, and love.

I admire you, he'd said. Simple words, but she felt she'd never received higher praise. Suddenly she was someone special despite her ordinary appearance and her far from ordinary upbringing. She'd never considered Ian needing something so simple as a friend. She'd never considered him needing *her*.

*You*, whispered a wormwood voice in her mind, *and the other woman who shares his bed*.

She pulled back her hands as if they'd been dipped in fire. "We can never be friends," she said hoarsely. "Never."

The disappointment in his eyes cut her to the heart.

"Why not?" he asked with soft determination.

*Because you're in love with someone else!* Jill tried, but found she couldn't even begin to put that painful reality into words. "Because . . . because I'll regret it. Maybe not today or tomorrow, but soon and for the rest of my—oh, God, now I'm even beginning to sound like this movie."

Bright rainbows had turned as stark and hard as the black and white world around her. Like an animal struggling to get free of a trap, she pulled herself away from him and slipped between two nearby couples into the concealing safety of the crowd. She heard him call out her name, but she didn't look back. Instead, she wove her way through the sea of close-packed nightclubbers, blinking back tears that had nothing to do with the cigarette smoke. Uncaring, she pushed on, ignoring everything around her, until she reached the front of the crowd.

She saw, for the first time, the nightclub band.

Their music was from the forties. Their champagne-white suits were from the forties. The trumpets and clarinets they played on were from the forties. But their Jamaican hats and Rastafarian dreadlocks were definitely from the nineties.

# NINE

"Einstein," Jill murmured as she stared at the band. "It's got to be a message from Einstein." Her spirits soared. It was the first clue she'd seen since she entered the virtual environment, and it meant that the AI computer was still alive. At least, she hoped that's what it meant.

She approached the bandstand cautiously. *Blend in*, she reminded herself. *After all, they may not want to talk to strange—*

"Be you Jillian Polanski?" the band leader asked.

*Then again, I could be wrong.* "Yes, I'm Jill. Do you know what's happened to Einstein? Can you tell me where he is?"

The Jamaican shook his head sadly, his natty dreadlocks swinging. "Ah, pretty lady, I be wishin' I could. But dis mon be only a partially realized spacial rendering program, don't ya know. My working-storage area can't hold dat much information. But this I know—dat little Einstein, he be in big trouble."

"What kind of trouble?" a deep, British-accented voice asked.

Startled, Jill turned to find the doctor standing close behind her. "How did you get through the crowd so fast?"

A corner of Sinclair's stern mouth curved up. "You aren't the only one capable of behaving like a water buffalo. Now," he continued as he faced the bandleader, "what kind of trouble is Einstein in?"

"Huge trouble, mon. Big as whale," the bandleader warned. "Einstein programmed me to tell you not to come after him. Too dangerous—for him, for you, and for your pretty lady. Better you leave him be."

"But we've come so far," Jill cried. "You've got to tell us how to find him."

"Like I said, I don't know where he be. Now, my information dispensing subroutine be at an end, so I'll be sayin' good-bye to ya both." And with those disheartening words he tipped his multipatterned hat and turned back to his band.

"But you're all we've got," Jill said, her voice dwindling to a whisper. They'd come so far—only to run full tilt into another blind alley. Only this time she'd allowed herself to hope. She looked up at Ian, not even attempting to hide the disappointment in her eyes. "We can't give up now, can we?"

"Not if I have anything to say about it," he promised. Striding forward, he grasped the bandleader's arm and spun him around to face him. "Listen, I built this bloody machine, and I know that every called program in this topology has to have had a point of origination. You may not be able to tell me where Einstein is now, but you can damn well tell me where he was when he brought you online."

"Well, you don't got to be such a nasty man about it," the bandleader complained. "Me start command came from the airport. Now, if you'll pardon dis mon, I got to play some music."

"By all means," Ian said, releasing his arm. He returned to Jill, expecting to see a smile on her face. Instead, he saw that her jaw was still drawn tight in worry, and a tiny crease of distress had appeared on her brow. He had an intense, extremely unscientific urge to kiss away that crease. *For God's sake, the woman can't even stomach the thought of being friends with you.*

"Ian, the airport's miles out of town. We'll never reach it in time."

She lifted her eyes to his, her beautiful, expressive eyes that were filled with compassion—for everyone but him. He ignored the sting of disappointment, reminding himself that he had no practical use for compassion in his efficient, ordered life. "Recently Sadie and I have done some research into the practice of transporting people within the virtual environment. Theoretically it should work."

"Theoretically?"

"Well, we haven't exactly tested it yet. And there

is the danger that we'll rematerialize in one of the environment's solid objects. But I'm willing to try it if you are." He stretched out his hand, offering her his upturned palm. "Are you game, Ms. Polanski?"

For a moment she simply stared at his hand. Then her lips curled into a soft ghost of a smile and she raised her eyes to his, meeting his gaze with the undaunted courage that had made him respect her more than any woman he'd ever known.

"Try and stop me, Doctor," she challenged him as she slipped her hand in his. "Just try."

It was not like Jill's other transitions. One second she was standing in the noisy, crowded nightclub; the next she was surrounded by the vast fog-cloaked emptiness of the Casablanca airport. Her senses reeled from the startling change, and she stumbled, clinging to the nearest object at hand for support. Which just happened to be the lapels of a raincoat covering a broad, muscular chest.

"Jillie, are you all right?"

*Jillie.* Why did he have to say her name like that, in a way that played along her skin like a virtuoso performing piano scales? And why couldn't she seem to find the energy to extract herself from her intimate position against his chest?

"I . . . I guess we made it."

"Presumably," he agreed, raising his hand to thump the metal skin of a nearby airplane wing. "We're at an airport. But where the devil did all this fog come from? It's rarely this thick on the Thames, and Morocco is a desert country."

"Casablanca is a port city. Besides, the fog is part of the movie. It adds to the romance and mystery."

"There's nothing mysterious about water condensation," he stated bluntly. "And romance is no excuse for inaccuracy. I'll have to speak to Sadie about this."

*A crustacean. Without the shell.* Sinclair may have been cast in the part of the romantic hero, but inside he was still Dr. Doom. She pulled herself out of his arms, trying not to notice how drop-dead gorgeous he looked in the well-worn raincoat and sloping fedora Sadie had given him. *Okay, so the guy could give Bogart macho lessons. That doesn't mean I'm going to just swoon into his arms.*

She turned away, conveniently forgetting that she'd already done just that. "Control, how much time have we got left?"

"Twelve minutes and ten seconds," Felix replied. "Better get a move on."

"No kidding. But where do we start?" The airport was much larger than it looked on the movie screen, and the layers of fog concealed much of it from view. To their left was the airport office, its sole light casting eerie shadows through the shifting gray curtain. To their right was a line of planes, silent and empty as a row of ghosts. She rubbed her hands along her arms, shivering with apprehension. The last time she'd felt this way, an orc had stepped out of the trees. . . .

"The office," Ian stated, interrupting her thoughts. "The light makes it an energy source. Einstein would need energy to transmit a program." He settled his hat firmly on his head and started to walk toward the office, motioning for her to follow. "This way, Ms. Polanski."

She obeyed—she didn't have much choice. Her only alternative was to be left standing alone and unprotected in the middle of a shadowed, fogbound runway. But as she hurried to catch up with him, watching his powerful strides and the easy swing of his hips, she wondered if she wasn't rushing from one dangerous situation to another. The doctor's potent physical presence was quickly whittling away at her resolve. And, virtual projection or not, she was only human.

"Nothing." Jill gave the clutter of papers strewn across the office floor a dejected kick. "There's nothing here at all."

"We still have five minutes," Ian commented as he continued to rifle through a nearby file cabinet. "Keep looking."

"Why? So your simulator can measure my frustration level? So your diodes can digitize my failure? You're only failing an experiment. But I'm failing . . . a friend."

She walked over to the office door and looked out toward the dark, dismal blackness of the airfield, feeling frustrated in ways she couldn't even begin to name. *It's not just Einstein that's making me crazy. It's Ian, and the way I feel about him. I don't like it. I don't want it. But it's there no matter what I do. And it's getting worse.*

"Jill."

She didn't turn around, not when he said her name, not when she heard the file drawer close and the sound of his footsteps coming up behind her. She hugged her arms protectively to her body, feeling more vulnerable than she ever had in her life.

"Jill, contrary to popular opinion, I do have a heart. I know how much Einstein means to you, and I won't stop searching until I find him. If I have to examine every cubic inch of his internal matrix, I'll find him. That's a promise."

His warm words brushed by her ear, melting her in intimate, erotic places. His virtual seduction technique was every bit as effective as the real thing. *And*, she reminded herself, *every bit as false*. She balled her hands into fists and spun around to face him, fighting to hang on to her anger like a sinner fights to hang on to her soul. "And what would you know about promises? You make and break them on a regular basis. You say you want to be my friend, but a friend doesn't pretend to care about you when he really cares about someone else. When he's *living* with someone else."

She looked into his dark eyes, hoping to see at least a trace of guilt. Instead, she saw only confusion, and concern. "What in blazes are you talking about?"

"I'm talking about the woman who called Marsha's looking for you. The one you live with. And I think it's pretty low of you to try to add another notch to your bedpost when that bed is occupied by someone el—Ian, don't you dare smile!"

He took her by the shoulders, forcing her to remain facing him. "Jill, I confess I do live with a woman, but she's my *housekeeper*."

"Housekeeper?" Jill repeated in a small voice.

Ian nodded, still grinning. "And just for the record, Partridge was also my nanny."

*His nanny!* Jill knew she'd probably made a complete fool of herself, but it somehow it didn't matter. Something cracked open inside her, a hard shell of resistance that had been born during her gypsy childhood and nurtured ever since. She looked up at Ian, seeing the gentle warmth in his smile, feeling it wash over her like yellow sunshine. For the first time she let herself believe in his gentleness, to trust him —and toppled into love with him with a force that took her breath away. "Ian," she breathed shakily, "I—"

"Vell, English, we meet again," said a heavily accented voice behind her.

*No, it can't be.* But as Jill whirled around, she saw that it not only could be, it was. Standing in the office doorway was the Nazi officer who'd threatened to shoot her at the nightclub. And once again his lethal-looking Luger was pointed directly at her heart.

"Not again," she groaned. "We already told you —we don't have your stupid letters."

"So you said," the Nazi agreed with a menacing smile. "But here you are at the airport. Why would you be here if you did not have the letters?"

"Because—oh, it's a long story. Ian, can't Sadie zap this loser out of the topology?"

"Not before he could get a bullet off, I'm afraid," the doctor admitted. He raised his head, his eyes narrowing as he looked at the storm trooper. "Look, if I tell you where the letters are, will you let the woman go?"

"No! I won't go. Not without you."

"Don't be a bloody fool. This way at least one of us gets out safely."

"I don't care," she cried, turning back to the officer. "He doesn't know where the letters are. Neither of us does."

"Too bad," the Nazi said with an indifferent shrug. "Zen I will have to kill you both."

He calmly cocked his weapon and leveled it at her heart. Good grief, the odious twerp was really going to kill her! *It's not fair*, her mind shouted. *Rick and Ilsa had Paris, but Ian and I never had anything.* She glanced up at Ian, wanting to tell him how she felt, to just say it once before she died. "Ian, I l—"

She never finished the sentence. Instead, she was grabbed from behind and shoved unceremoniously to the ground. The gun went off, missing her by a clear foot. But her relief vanished as she saw Ian launch himself at the Nazi.

"No!" she shouted, but by the time she said it, it was too late. Ian and the officer were locked in a down and dirty struggle, fighting for the gun the soldier still held.

"Ian!" she cried, feeling more helpless than she ever had in her life. She made a grab for the Nazi's boot, but the bastard kicked out, narrowly missing her face.

"Control, get her out of here!" Ian commanded. *"Now!"*

"Not without you!" But even as she said it, the world around her began to run together, like a watercolor in the rain. She was being pulled out of the topology whether she liked it or not. "Dammit, Sadie, I can't leave. I've got to help him!"

But Sadie didn't listen. Despite Jill's protests, the Casablanca world around her faded into nothing, shifting to the sightless black of the inside surface of her HMD visor. The last thing she heard was the gunshot.

"Ian!" She threw back the visor's hood and attacked the clasps on the harness, working furiously despite her still-unsteady fingers and the tears that brimmed in her eyes. With the clasps finally undone, she bolted from the harness, tearing several delicate nodes from their computer connections as she did so. She would have torn them all out if it meant getting free more quickly. She slammed her palm against the internal door switch. The door slid up, and she ducked through without waiting for it to open the whole way. *Ian.*

Outside, she ran to the edge of the egg's small platform. She could see the other egg suspended in the middle of the simulator's steel scaffolding. It was less than twenty feet away from her, but it might have been on the moon for all the good it did her. Between them was empty air—and a sheer drop to the laboratory floor below.

The egg's door was still sealed shut. She closed her eyes and leaned her head against the scaffolding, fighting the bitter helplessness that rose in her heart. "Let him be all right," she pleaded to the glass and metal monstrosity that surrounded her. "Please, please let him be all right."

A familiar whooshing noise made her open her eyes. She looked across to the other platform and saw the egg door open and a tall, achingly dear figure step through. Breathing heavily, he staggered against the side of the canister for support, clearly exhausted from his recent fight. Jill bit her lip, hoping to heaven exhaustion was all it was. "Ian?"

He turned at the sound of his name, jerking his head toward her. He shook his head as if to clear it, then focused on her as if he couldn't quite believe she was standing there. He tried to say something, but his ragged breathing prevented it. Instead, he looked at her with an intensity that stole her breath, even at that distance. Then, incredibly, he gave her a devilish wink.

There was no time for more. A nanosecond later Jill was surrounded by a swarm of busy technicians and paramedics, all of them stumbling over each other to insure her safety. Before she could say a word, she had a blood pressure cuff shoved up her arm and a thermometer stuffed into her mouth.

She caught sight of a familiar face and pulled the thermometer out despite the huffy displeasure of the nurse who had put it in. "Felix, who are all these people?"

"Sadie and I thought you might need some medical help when you got back," Felix said as he hunkered down beside her. "We called every medical resource person in the building."

"Looks like you called everyone in Miami." Then, seeing Felix's crestfallen face, she placed a comforting hand on his arm. "I'm sorry. You did the right thing. I'm just sorry it was all for nothing. We didn't find Einstein."

"No, but *we* did," he told her. "You weren't able to see it visually, but the topology overlay of the office was just stuffed with cryptic hexadecimal equations. We pinpointed the location in core and started downloading it even before you went. If Einstein's left us a message, we'll be able to decode it."

"Felix, that's wonderful," Jill said, giving her friend a congratulatory hug. "Wait until you tell Ian. He'll probably give you a raise."

"Oh, I told him. No raise, but he said he wanted to get working on the equations immediately. He already left the lab for his office."

"He left?" *Without seeing me? Without even checking to see if I was all right?*

Well, what did she expect? This was the real

world, not the sepia-toned virtual reality of *Casablanca*. She'd stepped out of Ilsa's designer clothes into her functional bodysuit. She'd stepped out of the glittering, romantic illusion into her commonplace, everyday life. Casablanca was a dream, and nothing that had happened there mattered in the real world.

Nothing—except for the little fact that she'd fallen in love with Ian Sinclair.

She felt a sharp stab of disappointment, which she quickly disguised with anger. "Well," she grumbled, "the least he could have done is thank me for trying to help him save his life."

"I think he might have," Felix said. He reached into his lab coat and pulled out a crumpled piece of paper. "He asked me to give you this."

She unfolded the note slowly. Inside was a scrawled sentence followed by a bold letter *S. Pick you up seven-thirty tonight.*

It was only a date. She'd be a fool to read more into it. Nevertheless, her spirits soared. She felt the disappointment drain out of her heart, replaced by all the colors of joy. In the make-believe world of the simulator she'd discovered the greatest truth of all—love.

But would her joy dissolve, like Casablanca's bogus fog, in the unforgiving light of reality?

# TEN

"I can't believe I let you talk me into this," Jill said as she studied herself in her full-length bedroom mirror.

"Why?" Marsha asked, coming over to stand beside her friend. "In the words of Billy Crystal, 'You look mahvelous.'"

*Mahvelous* was not the first word that sprung to Jill's mind. True, the dress Marsha had lent her was strikingly beautiful—a strapless black velvet sheath that wrapped her body like a glove. And Jill couldn't deny that the style Marsh had teased her brown hair into made it look less mediocre than usual. But underneath the dress and the big hair she was still plain, ordinary Jill Polanski. She felt like an ugly duckling, except that she knew she wasn't ever going to turn into a swan. She felt . . . dishonest.

"I don't know, Marsh," she said as she bent down to smooth her black silk stockings. "It's just not me."

"Well, whoever you are, Dr. Doom's gonna love you in that dress," her friend said practically. "And when he finds out you're wearing garters—"

"He's not going to find out," Jill promised as she glanced back to the mirror, feeling more and more unsure of herself. "Maybe this wasn't such a good idea."

"Trust me, it's the best idea I've ever had," Marsh stated confidently. "Now, where are your shoes?"

"Next to the dresser. But seriously—"

"Seriously?" Marsh repeated as she collected the sequined velvet high-heeled shoes from the bureau. "Seriously—I haven't seen you this wound up over something since . . . well, since we raided the bio building to free the lab mice." She walked back to the mirror and handed the heels to her friend, frowning in concern. "I don't get it, Jill. You've been on lots of dates. Why are you so nervous about this one?"

*Because I'm in love*, she repeated silently, not even able to trust Marsha with her terrible, glorious secret. She was in love—desperate, passionate, aching love—with a man who didn't know the meaning of the word. *Hopeless* didn't even begin to cover it.

"He's kind of stuffy," Marsha continued, apparently not noticing her friend's silence. "Are you worried he's not going to be good in bed?"

"What? No, of course not! Good God, that's got nothing to do with—"

"Then are you worried *you* aren't going to be

good?" Marsh asked, undaunted. "Because if you are, you shouldn't be. Sometimes it takes a while to work the mechanics out—like who likes to be on top and stuff—but after a few times, I'm sure—"

"Marsha," Jill pleaded, blushing to the roots of her hair. Images of Ian in both of the positions her friend had mentioned flashed through her mind, increasing her embarrassment. "We haven't . . . I mean, Dr. Sinclair and I aren't—"

"Doing the nasty?" Marsha finished, smiling slyly. "I know that. But considering the amount of virtual and real kissing that's been going on between you two, I suspect it's only a matter of time. Anyway, I put a condom in your purse, just in case you two— oh, for heaven's sake, Jill, don't look so ticked off. It's not like you're a virgin or anything."

Well, not technically, Jill thought, her blush deepening. She'd had a brief physical relationship in college with one of her fellow environmentalists. But their few, largely disappointing sexual encounters had left her clueless as to what men wanted physically. She had no idea of what turned men on—except that she didn't seem to have any of it.

The doorbell rang, bringing all her thoughts, except panic, to a halt.

"Show time!" Marsha chorused, hustling her friend out the bedroom door toward the stairs. "Now, remember, I'll feed Merlin and lock up here. You just have a fun time."

*Fun?* Jill suspected Daniel had more fun facing the lion's den. Briefly she considered sending Marsha to the door with a message that she was sick or dead or something, but there were three very good reasons why she couldn't do that. One, matchmaker Marsha wouldn't agree to do it. Second, Ian probably wouldn't believe that she was really dead—especially when she showed up at the lab the following afternoon for their next episode in the simulator. And the third, the most damning reason of all, was that—despite her anxiety—she couldn't bear the thought of not seeing him.

She pulled open the door, smiling up at the place she expected his face to be—and lowered it in surprise when she saw that the man on the other side of the door wasn't Ian. "Who are you?"

"Rogers, ma'am," the shorter, considerably wider stranger answered. "I'm Dr. Sinclair's chauffeur. He's working on the simulator equations, and asked me to pick you up and drive you to his estate."

"Chauffeur?" Jill repeated in surprise. Then, as the words sunk in, she added in a strangled gasp, "*Estate?*"

"Dammit, the answer's here somewhere," Ian muttered as he studied the computer printouts strewn across his home office desk. Rows and rows of hexadecimal numbers littered the pages—machine code—mined whole from the very heart of Einstein's core. The bits and bytes translated to computer commands—a language as intricate and powerful as any medieval incantation. Change a number here, and you could talk to a person halfway around the world. Insert a calculation there, and you could fly to the moon. It was the sorcery of science, the spell of predictable magic. And somewhere in this ream of statistical wizardry was the digital key that would unlock the secret to Einstein's disappearance.

Ian's intercom buzzed.

"Rogers phoned from the car," a lyrical voice on the other end of the line informed him. "He just passed the front gate."

"Fine. I'll be down soon," Ian answered vaguely, his attention still focused on the printouts.

"You'll get downstairs this instant, you heartless bugger. You're the one who invited the poor lass to this mausoleum, and I'll not have you let her arrive here without a welcome."

Ian chuckled at the reprimand. He'd received similar chastisements since he was six years old, and knew they were delivered with more love than anger. "All right, Partridge," he said, depressing the intercom lever. "I'm coming down now."

He rose from his desk and stretched his cramped muscles. How long had he been sitting here? An hour? Two? Well, he'd better get used to it—he still had the lion's share of the data to sift through, most of which was stacked downstairs on the dining room table. There he and Jill could spread them out and study them in detail. Her knowledge of Einstein's internal matrix would be invaluable.

*Is that the only reason you wanted her here?*

Of course it was. His dining room was three

times as large as any of the conference cubicles at the office. And while his nineteenth-century ancestor's baronial banquet table hadn't been specifically constructed as an oversize work space, it would serve that purpose admirably. He and Ms. Polanski would be able to go over the printouts thoroughly, without any of the annoying distractions of the office. It made perfect, logical sense to invite her to his house.

*Just like it made perfect, logical sense to douse yourself in cologne.*

He hadn't *doused*. He'd merely put some on after he'd taken a shower, and changed into some comfortable clothes. And just because those clothes happened to be a black V-neck sweater and a pair of jeans that Partridge had told him "would keep a gel's attention focused somewhere other than his mind" . . . well, they were just the first things that came to hand.

*And I suppose your razor just came to hand as well. You never shave in the evening, but tonight you—*

"Enough!" he said aloud, as if a verbal reply could silence his nagging conscience. He gathered up the printouts on his desk and left his den, steering his course toward the stairway that led to the main vestibule and steering his mind back to the important matters at hand—locating Einstein and determining what sort of danger was threatening him. These were the quantifiable objectives, not analyzing what feelings he did or did not have for Ms. Jillian Polanski.

He reached the top of the stairway, pausing to

look down on the vestibule. The elegant creation of gold-veined marble and crystal chandeliers was the culmination of Samantha's considerable decorating talents. It was beautiful, magnificent, breathtaking—and as coldly sterile as the inside of a tomb.

Partridge had nicknamed it the Mausoleum, and had wanted to redecorate as soon as Samantha moved out. Ian, however, had resisted. The decor reminded him of his ex-wife, and the terrible mistake he'd made in marrying her. It reminded him to stick to science and leave the softer emotions to other, less-jaded men. It reminded him that he wasn't built for romance, even if his simulator had temporarily cast him in the role of a knight in shining armor, and a matinee idol. In the real world he was the solitary Dr. Doom, who lived alone in a house that resembled a mausoleum. And if the doctor occasionally fantasized about a pair of doe-brown eyes, a fierce, determined little chin, and a soft, incredibly kissable mouth, it was just his own rotten lu—

"Ohmigod!" said a startled voice from the vestibule below.

*She's here*, he thought, quickly dampening an unwanted surge of pleasure. He glanced down and saw Jillian step tentatively into the crystal room. She was wrapped in the most god-awful coat he'd ever seen, the engulfing material making her look young and vulnerable—and completely adorable. A soft smile tugged at his stern lips as he watched her wander like a lost sparrow through the glittering wonderland. *I could replicate this room in a heartbeat in my simulator, but there's no way on earth I could replicate her.*

Downstairs, Jill shivered as a familiar awareness tingled down her spine. It was almost as if Ian . . . but he wasn't there. *Good thing, too*, she thought as she glanced around at the incredible room. She'd known from the fact that Ian had a chauffeur that he was wealthy—but not *this* wealthy. She needed a few minutes to get used to the idea. Hell, she needed a few months.

People said money didn't matter, but she'd spent enough of her life without it to know better. Money made people different. She'd hoped to spend the evening finding out things she and Ian had in common, but the more she learned about the enigmatic scientist, the more glaring their differences became. The only thing that kept her from walking back out the door was the fact that Ian had invited her there. He must see their differences as clearly as she did, but he'd asked her because he wanted to try to build a relationship. What other reason could there be?

"It's about time you got here," said an unfamiliar voice on her right.

Jill turned toward the speaker, who was entering the front hall through the living room door. The woman was stoutly built and almost painfully plain, and the severe, high-collared dress she wore did little to improve her appearance. But while her looks were unremarkable, the welcome shining in her honest face was anything but. *This has got to be Partridge.* "Sorry. I didn't realize I was running late."

"Well, you are, and I don't just mean for dinner," Partridge said cryptically. She held Jill at arm's length and gave her a quick but thorough perusal. "Yes, you'll do. I understood you thought the doctor and I were shacking up together."

Jill blinked at the light-speed change of subject. "I didn't mean . . . that is, I misunderstood . . ."

"No need to apologize," Partridge said, patting Jill's arm comfortingly. "My boy excels at misunderstandings. Couldn't get the right words out if you tied his tongue to a truck and dragged them out of him. Why, I remember one time when he was just a little shaver he—"

"That will do," commanded a stern voice from above.

*Ian!* Jill looked up, and saw him standing at the top of the gilded staircase, looking like a black king in a glittering white palace. His presence washed over her like a dark wave, stretching and tightening her body in delicious, frightening places. She swallowed, her mouth suddenly gone dry as dust. *Just remember that he was the one who invited you here*, she told herself as she watched him start down the stairway. *Under that cool, confident façade he must be feeling just as nervous as I—*

And then she saw the printouts.

"I'm glad you could come on such short notice," he said as he reached the bottom of the stairs. "I've got most of the data from Einstein's core dump stacked in the dining room. We can start analyzing the figures immediately."

"You asked me here . . . to analyze figures?"

"Yes, and we'd better get to it," he said brusquely, glancing at his watch. "We're already running late—"

"Oh, for Lord's sake," Partridge interrupted. "Can't you even wait for the lass to take off her coat?"

"There's no need," Jill said quietly. "I'd like to keep it on." She had no intention of revealing the dress she hid beneath it—or the dreams that had just been shattered into dust. Ian had asked her there to look at core dumps, not to romance her. She'd misread his motives so completely, she could have laughed aloud—if her heart hadn't been breaking.

*Well, this is the last time*, she promised herself as she lifted her chin and followed Ian toward the dining room. She'd been fooled by the doctor's feelings for her before, but she wouldn't let it happen again. He could stay behind his hard, emotionless façade till doomsday. He could rot in this beautiful, soulless house for all she cared. Once they'd found Einstein, she was going back to her job at Sheffield, where she'd never have to see him again.

And maybe, if she worked very hard at it, she'd forget how much she loved him.

Dinner was a disaster. No matter what they said to each other, it lead to a battle, striking sparks between them like iron on flint. Einstein's indecipherable data dumps only added to their frustration, giving them even more excuses to argue. By the end of the meal even "pass the salt" had become a bone of contention.

"I don't see why you're so upset," Ian said as he headed for the living room, hoping the change in location would defuse the tension between them. "I merely said that studies showed that most Americans use too much salt—"

"Great, now you're trying to dictate my diet," Jill snapped. "Thanks, Doctor, but I've been eating just fine on my own for years. I don't need you to tell me how."

"I wasn't—oh, what's the use?" He ran his fingers through his hair, pushed to the edge by her argumentative attitude. He'd promised her he'd find Einstein. He'd asked her here to help him—something he thought she'd appreciate. But instead she stood in the opposite corner of the living room, like a fighter about to enter the ring. He'd gone several rounds with her already, and didn't relish another battle. What in blazes was the matter with her? "I could use a drink," he stated, turning to the wet bar. "Can I get you one?"

"No, thank you," she replied with brittle politeness.

"Suit yourself." He splashed a healthy portion of straight scotch into a glass, foregoing the ice. He hadn't been this worked up over a female since— hell, he'd *never* been this worked up over a female. He took a long pull of liquor, relishing its clean, honest bite. Some things, at least, could be depended on. "I wish you would tell me why you're so upset."

"Why, so you can log it with the rest of your test data?"

He spun around, biting back a word he hadn't used since adolescence. "I don't . . . I asked you here to help find out what happened to Einstein. I thought that was what you wanted."

"Of course that's what I wanted. What else would I want?"

She balled her hands into fists, shivering with barely contained ire. Her anger was a puzzle—and Ian was a master at solving puzzles. He leaned back against the wet bar, studying her for some clue to her inexplicable emotion. But all he saw was fury—desperate, anguished fury—like a bird beating its wings to get out of a trap she has no hope of escaping.

"I'd like to go home now," she said suddenly.

Ian straightened, startled not so much by her statement, but by his fierce, gut-level reaction to it. *Don't let her go. Not now. Not ever.* He took another pull on his drink, trying to make sense of his own chaotic feelings. "Of course, you can leave anytime you want to, but—"

"No *buts* about it. I've endured this evening for as long as I intend to. I've endured *you*, Doctor," she said, turning toward the door to the vestibule. "I want to go home."

"Well, you're not going yet." Pushed past the limit, he slammed down his glass and crossed the room in three strides. He took her arm, grasping the material of her horrible raincoat, anchoring her in place. "You're not leaving until we have this out."

"Like hell," she cried, struggling against him. It wasn't much of a struggle—Ian had ten times her strength, and he was fully prepared to use it. But Jill knew she had to get away. This place was suffocating her. *He* was suffocating her. Desperate, she untied the sash of her coat and slipped out of it, hoping to get past the front door and into the darkness before he could—

"Bloody hell!"

The shock of his voice brought her to a dead halt. She glanced back, and saw him staring at her as if she'd suddenly been stripped stark naked. Oh, God, she thought, slowly turning her gaze downward. The dress. She'd forgotten about the damning dress.

She swallowed and spoke into the cavernous silence. "It's Marsha's," she offered.

"It's not Marsha's body," he replied. His intense gaze stroked over her, burning her wherever it touched. "What possessed you to wear it?"

*Possessed.* That was the word, all right. He possessed her thoughts for longer than she could remember, owning her emotions, stealing into her dreams. This afternoon she'd admitted to herself that she loved him, but the damage had been done long before that. He'd been in her mind from the moment she'd met him, and in her heart for nearly as long. God knows she wanted him out of both—

and she'd tried! But she was obsessed beyond reason with the dark, enigmatic scientist. And the bastard didn't give a damn about her.

"Call Rogers," she demanded. "I want to leave."

"Jill, we need to talk—"

"I don't want to talk with you!" She turned away, mortified that she was beginning to cry. She had to get out of there—fast. Even a block of wood like Ian would eventually figure out why she had worn the dress. And then she'd die, she'd just die. "If you won't call Rogers, I'll take a cab. There's got to be a phone in here some—"

Her words ended abruptly as Ian caught her wrist from behind and spun her roughly around to face him. He stared at her for one heart-stopping second. Then his mouth came down on hers. Hard.

It was a ravaging kiss, demanding and receiving the full measure of her passion. Resistance wasn't even a remote option. His lips consumed her, laving hot caresses on her cheeks and throat, devouring her in ways that left her aching and breathless, and eager for more. When he finally lifted his head, she sagged against him, clinging to him as she fought for breath. She nuzzled the open throat of his sweater, drinking in the musky smell of his skin. "Doctor," she said shakily, "you present a very persuasive argument for staying."

His deep chuckle was almost as sexy as his kisses. "My pleasure, Ms. Polanski," he murmured, stroking her hair. "Why in blazes didn't you take off that coat sooner?"

"Printouts."

"What printouts?"

She sighed, reluctantly lifting her head to meet his questioning gaze. "The ones you were carrying when you came downstairs. You made it clear that this was a business arrangement—period."

"Yes, I suppose I did," he agreed, smiling grimly. "I was so busy convincing myself that I wasn't interested in you that I convinced you too." He shifted her slightly, nestling her head in the curve of his throat. "Sometimes I behave like a bloody idiot."

Against his neck her mouth pulled into a smile. "Only sometimes?" Then, turning serious, she asked quietly, "You're not doing this out of . . . pity, are you?"

His arms tightened protectively around her. "If you think this is pity, I must be more out of practice than I—"

His comment was cut short by the sharp, insistent wail of his beeper. "Lord, not now!"

"Do you have to answer it?"

"Unfortunately, yes," he said, grimacing at the number displayed on the pager. "It's my custom-parts manufacturer in Germany. He needs some measurements . . . Jill, I've got to take this upstairs. It shouldn't—it won't take long. We need to talk—"

"I know," she said softly. "I'll be here when you get back. I promise."

After Ian left, she returned to the living room and sat demurely on the couch to wait—but she bounced up a second later. She couldn't sit still, not after what had happened, not with all the colors in the world boiling inside her. She placed her fingers against her lips, still tender from the ardent pressure of his kisses. She felt as if she could fly. *Okay, so we're different. He's filthy rich, and I'm a farm girl from Nebraska. But differences can sometimes make a relationship stronger. Anything's possible as long as we have love in common.* . . .

"My boy's quite taken with you."

Jill looked up. Partridge had entered the living room and was observing her intently. *A lioness and her cub,* Jill thought, loving him all the more for the affection he shared with this plain, good woman. "Well, I'm sort of taken with him too," she confessed.

Partridge nodded succinctly. She gave the rest of the room a quick glance, and immediately focused on Ian's discarded glass. She walked to the wet bar and rinsed it out with an efficiency that defined English nannies everywhere. "That's good. It's about time my boy started seeing a nice, well-brought-up young gel instead of flash bits like that creature he married."

Well-brought-up, Jill thought with a sad smile. *Partridge, if you only knew* . . .

"Now, don't you think I'm telling tales behind her back," she continued as she traveled around the room, plumping pillows and straightening ornaments. "I've said the same to Samantha many a time.

I knew from the first she was no good for my boy, that she was only after his money and his title."

"Title? You mean his doctorates?"

"Lord, no, lass. His *hereditary* title. The barony."

"Barony?" Jill repeated hollowly. "Ian's a *baron*?"

"The Baron of Carlisle, one of the most revered families in all Britain. He's eighty-ninth in line to the throne," she added with a pride that indicated she considered him far superior to the other eighty-eight. She turned and pointed to a picture on the wall, a beautifully framed lithograph from the last century that fit right in with Samantha's royally appointed decorations. "That's his castle."

Jill moved toward the picture like a man walking in front of a firing squad. She studied the impressive structure, trying not to let her growing despair show on her face. *Rich was bad enough, but he's got a damn castle. . . .*

Partridge prattled on, cheerfully relating stories of Ian's privileged youth on the castle grounds. Jill nodded politely, but her frozen smile went no farther than her lips. No doubt good-hearted Partridge thought she was adding to Ian's stature in Jill's eyes. She had no idea she was helping to dig his grave.

Jill could tell the difference between fantasy and reality. She knew that outside of storybooks and simulator programs, true love rarely conquered all. Her knowledge of royalty was limited to what she'd read in the headlines of the supermarket tabloids, but she was quite certain that a wealthy, titled nobleman wasn't likely to enter into a serious relationship with a woman who'd spent the first ten years of her life fleeing from creditors and angry wives through half the states in the Union. A woman whose capricious mother's list of lovers read like the Miami phone book.

A woman who didn't even know the name of her own father.

# ELEVEN

"I still think you should let Rogers drive you home, miss," Partridge said as she peered through the front-door pane at the waiting taxi. "Or at least wait until the doctor comes back downstairs."

"I can't wait. I've got . . . work," Jill said, almost wincing at the lameness of the excuse. Calling Instant Cab had been a cowardly thing to do, but she had to get away from here. She knew she'd promised Ian, but that was before . . .

"Please give the doctor my apologies, and thank him for inviting me to dinner. It was very kind of him."

Partridge's eyes narrowed with canny concern. "I don't believe he did it to be kind."

Jill turned away from the woman's scrutiny. *Trust me, Partridge, if you knew the truth, you wouldn't want me anywhere near "your boy."* In Ian's arms she'd felt like Cinderella at the ball, but it was time to get back to reality. And as she looked down, she saw that neither of her very unglasslike shoes were missing. *Dreams*, she told herself as she gave her raincoat belt a ruthless tug. *Stupid, empty dreams.* She started for the door. "Partridge, please tell the doctor that I . . . that I'll see him at the simulator tomorrow afternoon."

She hurried to the taxi without a backward glance, eager to get as far away from Ian's house— and Ian—as she could. He'd be hurt by her sudden departure, but he'd get over it. She wasn't nearly so confident about herself. She needed to be alone, to think about her future—a practical future that didn't include stern, soft-hearted, irresistibly sexy scientists who lured women into loving them without telling them they were royalty in disguise.

She slipped into the enveloping darkness of the cab. The back of her legs rubbed against the slick leather seats worn smooth by a thousand unknown occupants. She glanced over at the shimmering wonderland of Ian's house, realizing that she, too, was slipping back into the anonymity of her safe, ordinary life. A life without passion, without love, *without Ian* . . .

"Miss? Señorita! I asked where you want to go."

Jill raised her head and met the worried stare of her mustachioed, sharp-eyed Cuban driver. She'd been so lost in her thoughts that she hadn't heard the man's repeated questions—so lost that she hadn't even closed the cab door behind her. *Great, at this rate I'll be sitting here all night.* "I'm sorry. I guess I wasn't listening."

"Pretty lady like you shouldn't frown so much," he commented sagely.

Jill opened her mouth to reply, but was interrupted by a familiar baritone. "I agree."

*No, it can't be.* But as Ian sandwiched his tall form into the limited space of the cab's backseat, she realized that it was. "Ian! You can't— Look, I told Partridge—"

"You told Partridge to tell me you were leaving. You just didn't know she'd use the intercom to do it. Now, stop all this foolishness and come back in the house."

*And back to your reason-numbing kisses? I don't think so.* "I'm going home."

"Fine," he replied curtly with a tight, not altogether pleasant smile. He yanked the car door shut behind him. "I'll come with you."

"Like hell you will—" Jill began, but Ian interrupted her.

"Would you rather talk about this tomorrow? In front of Felix, Sadie, and the rest of the department?"

She wouldn't, and he knew it. She remembered how the staff had whispered and giggled when they'd seen the video of her and Ian's cyberkiss—imagine what they'd say if they had a real relationship to gossip about. "It's all right," she told the understandably perplexed driver. "But the gentleman will be taking this cab back."

The gentleman merely smiled.

Jill gave the driver her address, and the taxi started down the driveway. She shoved herself into the farthest corner of the seat, wanting to put as much distance between herself and Ian as possible. It wasn't easy. The taxi's backseat wasn't large to begin with, and Ian took up most of it. No matter how she turned, she couldn't avoid touching Ian's knee with her own. The contact was electric. *Damn him. Why did he have to follow me in the first place?*

*And why did I let him?*

The cab had turned off the well-lit driveway and onto the empty country road. Darkness filled the car like ink in a well, yet Jill could feel Ian's intense eyes watching her, piercing her. She shifted nervously in the seat, a move that unfortunately brought more of her leg into contact with Ian's. Beneath the form-fitting jeans she felt the hard muscles of his calves, the coiled energy of a panther waiting to strike. *God.* "I'm sorry I left without telling you," she said truthfully. "I . . . I remembered I had work to finish."

Ian gave a snort of disbelief. "That's what Partridge told me. I didn't buy it then, and I don't buy it now. You weren't just leaving—you were running away."

"I wasn't running away," she stated. But, of course, she had been. Retreat was preferable to telling him the truth about herself. Then and now. "Listen, I don't owe you an explanation. I don't owe you a damn th—"

Her sentence stopped abruptly as she swiped her

arm for emphasis, and inadvertently knocked over her purse. The contents spilled onto the seat between them. *Perfect*, she thought as she hurried to stuff the items back into her handbag. *At least things can't get any worse.*

But they did. Ian reached over to help her, closing his fist around several of the scattered objects. The darkness obscured their identity, but there was no mistaking the telltale crunch of foil.

"What the—?"

"Marsha," she explained weakly, grabbing the condom out of his hand and stuffing it into her purse. "I wasn't . . . I mean, I didn't . . . let's just pretend this whole evening never happened."

"I can't do that, Ms. Polanski. Nor," he added with lethal softness, "would I want to."

*Neither do I*, she thought helplessly, *but I have to.* A relationship with Ian could only break her heart. He was right—she *had* been running away. But instead of escaping from him, she was closer to him than ever. The small backseat was filled with him— his body, his smell, his heat—she was suffocating from it. She'd never been so aware of a man's sexuality before. Or of her own. She swallowed, trying desperately to rein back her careening emotions. "I think it would be better for everyone if we didn't see each other anymore."

"That's not an answer." He grasped her wrist, pulling her closer with a cruel and gentle strength. "Why, Jillie? What did I do to drive you away?"

The bewilderment in his voice split her heart.

"Oh, Ian, it's not like that. It's—" She stopped as the cab passed a streetlight, and she caught sight of their driver's curious stare in the rearview mirror. Honestly, just once couldn't they have a discussion without an audience? She dropped her voice to whisper. "I left because—"

"Why are you whispering?"

Jill inched closer. "I'm whispering because—"

"Are you feeling all right?" asked the infinitely practical doctor. "Have you got laryngitis?"

"I don't—argh!" Exasperated, Jill leaned against him and whispered directly into his ear. "I haven't got laryngitis. I just don't want to share our personal business with a nosy cabdriver. Can you hear me now?"

After a meaningful pause he answered, "Yes."

It wasn't what he said, but the way he said it—as if he were fighting for breath to speak even that short word. Jill realized how close they were, and how her torso was pressed full against the solid wall of his chest. Layers of clothing separated them, but they might have been naked by the way her breasts molded to his hard planes of muscle, aching with a delicious sensitivity. *They might have been naked . . .*

"Maybe this wasn't a good idea," she whispered shakily, finding that she was also short of breath.

"Nonsense," he answered gruffly. "We're scientists—our minds control our bodies, not the other way around. Do go on."

*Well, if he can stand it, so can I.* Determined, she willed herself not to feel the threads of fire weaving through her arms and legs, and wherever else her body touched his. She pulled herself up to his ear, trying to ignore the way the wonderful scent of his hair tickled her nose. "I left because there are things in my past that you don't know about. Our backgrounds are so different. . . ."

He turned toward her ear, brushing his jaw against the sensitive skin of her neck as he did so.

"I'm trying to point out the differences between us. I'm—" she began to say.

The taxi hit a pothole, throwing Jill off balance. She would have hit the seat in front of her if Ian hadn't caught her and pulled her back. "Bloody hell," he cursed at the driver, "can't you watch where you're going?"

"Pardon, señor," the apologetic cabbie muttered.

Jill barely heard the exchange. Cradled against Ian's broad chest, she felt safe and protected—and ridiculously content. She was vaguely aware of the shift in her position—that somehow she'd ended up sitting in Ian's lap, with his right hand resting on her stockinged thigh just below her hemline. The darkness and the motion of the cab created a strangely separate atmosphere, as if she and Ian were in a space apart from the rest of the world—a world where she was warm, and safe, and cherished. It was a fantasy, an illusion as false as the topological overlays in the simulator. But she couldn't seem to help herself from nuzzling closer to him, and breathing in his clean, incredibly masculine scent.

"Jillie," Ian murmured against her hair.

His rough-textured fingers stroked up her thigh, trailing tremors of delight across her ultrasensitive skin. Passion ignited within her. She'd had a taste of his caresses earlier that evening, but it was nothing like this. This was slow and steamy, as if he intended to make love to every part of her. *Every* part. She groaned, knowing she couldn't want this, knowing it was poison to want this. "Ian, we can't . . ."

His deep chuckle sent delicious shivers down her spine. "When I was a child, I lived in a castle that has been in my family for centuries. It's cold and damp, and it's so crowded with the trophies of my ancestors that there's no room left for the living. I've lived among the dead for so long, I'd forgotten what it was like to be alive." He leaned closer, giving her earlobe a seductive nip. "Or I had, until a certain spitfire barreled into my office and gave me hell for not recycling."

Jill's eyes widened in surprise. "But that was my first day!"

Against her hair she felt his mouth curve into a smile. "And it's been torture being near you ever since. Do you know how long I've wanted to kiss you? Do you know how long I've wanted to touch you like this?"

His hand claimed her inner thigh. Desire exploded through her like a bursting star. "You can't," she gasped as she glanced at the silhouette of the cabbie's head. "We can't—"

His leather-soft voice was as seductive as his touch. "Let me, Jillie. Just once let me touch you the way I've wanted to, the way I've dreamed about. . . ."

His hand followed his words, moving higher up, until he reached the bare skin above her garter-secured stockings. She moaned, pressing her mouth against his shoulder to kill the sound. *He wanted me from the start*, she thought, feeling a bright bitter-sweet longing well up inside her. *He wants the person he thinks I am.*

She was crazy to let him do this, and not only because of the cabbie. Their passion didn't change her past, or his. This was illusion—a dark, hot, sin-fully wonderful illusion as unreal as cyberspace. She needed to end this—now. But as his fingers began to stroke the naked flesh of her inner thigh, she knew she couldn't summon the will to stop him even if she'd wanted to. Being touched by Ian was her fan-tasy too.

She gave herself to him. Instinctively she moved against his hand, picking up the rhythm of his love-making. His strong fingers stroked magic through her, arousing her to a fever pitch. When he cupped her she buried her face in the hollow of his neck, groaning as a tidal wave of pleasure ripped through her.

"I want you," he growled. "I want you hot and naked and under me. Say you want it too."

Want it? She was dying for it. She was mad for him, burning for a fulfillment only he could provide. From the waist up she was a perfect lady. From the waist down she was moving to the rhythm of his incredible caress, wild as a bitch in heat. She couldn't take much more. She couldn't imagine stopping.

"Say it," he commanded, his voice thick with the strain of his own passion. He bent closer, his lips hovering torturing inches above hers. "I don't care if it's true or not. Tell me you want me."

*Not true? How can he doubt it?* Her body was proving how much she wanted him, how much she loved him. Her love for him was the one true thing about her. It was also the one thing she couldn't bear to admit. To be this close, then to see the passion die in his eyes when she told him the truth about herself . . . that really would kill her. "Ian, I can't—"

The taxi jerked to a halt. Turning her head, Jill saw the lights of her town house condominium. The ride was over. And the fantasy.

Afterward she was never entirely sure how Ian untangled their bodies so quickly, or how he managed to set her on the other side of the seat with her coat demurely pulled down over her legs before the cabbie had a chance to switch off the meter and turn around. "We're here, Señorita. And the señor—will he be going back?"

"Yes," Ian stated before she had a chance to reply. "The señor will."

He opened the door and helped her out, but there was no warmth in either his touch or his expression. His mask was back in place, the steel façade that made people view him as cold and distant. But Jill knew that behind his impassive exterior beat a passionate, vulnerable heart. A heart just as capable of being broken as her own.

There couldn't be anything permanent between them, she knew that. But she also knew that she owed him the truth as to why not. He'd rescued her from an orc and a Nazi, and most recently from the knowing leer of a curious cabdriver. She couldn't let him leave believing that he was the reason she'd left, that somehow he'd driven her away. She curled her fingers around the hand that rested on the door handle. "Ian, what you wanted me to say in the cab . . . it's true."

For the space of several heartbeats, nothing happened. Then he turned his hand palm-up and laced his fingers through her own. Their gazes locked, and for a precious moment there wasn't a sound in the world but their hushed breathing, and the pounding rhythm of their hearts.

"You can drive on, cabbie," Ian said without taking his eyes from Jill's. "The señor will be staying."

# TWELVE

She walked into the shadowed darkness of her living room, seeing the familiar shapes of her furniture, the glint of the pale moon through her sliding glass door. This home was a haven for her, an island of peace in a crazy, chaotic world. But peace evaporated as she heard a footstep behind her.

"Would you like me to turn on a light?" he asked quietly.

"No," she said. It was easier in the darkness, easier to confess the truth about her upbringing. She hugged her arms to her body, a neat trick in the enveloping coat she still wore. Still turned away from him, she spoke, hoping that the perfect words would just tumble out of her mouth. But all that came out was "Would you like some tea?"

She heard the smile in his voice. "Not right now."

*Stupid, of course he doesn't want tea.* She grimaced,

painfully aware of how inept she'd sounded. But she really couldn't be anything but inept about this. She'd never invited a man into her house to . . . well, she never had. Movies and books always made it sound so easy, as natural as falling off a log. But she'd never felt more unnatural. She felt shy and awkward, and she hadn't a clue on how to proceed. "Well, how about some coffee?"

"What I'd *like* is for you to relax," he said as he came to stand behind her. "We're alone here. No simulator cameras, no cybertechs, no orcs, Nazis, or cabdrivers. It's just you and me. And truthfully," he admitted as he pressed a heated kiss on the back of her neck, "I'm almost as clueless about this procedure as you are."

*Yeah, sure.* "You were married for six years."

"I know about *sex.*" His voice grew hard, with a bitter edge that cut to her own heart. "Samantha had an insatiable appetite for physical pleasure. Trouble was, she didn't much care who she was doing it with. Men were interchangeable to her. Including her husband."

He sounded so remote, so alone. She turned in his arms, and saw that isolation mirrored in his eyes. For the first time she understood his remoteness, the reason he'd built a wall of facts and figures around his heart. She smiled softly, unafraid of his forbidding expression because she knew and loved the man behind it. "She's wrong, Doctor. You're definitely one of a kind."

The harshness left his expression. In the silvered

moonlight she watched his features soften, taking on the treasured gentleness she'd so rarely seen. Her breath caught in her throat as she saw the man she loved looking down at her without a trace of the barriers that had kept them apart for so long.

"You're rather special yourself," he said with a tenderness that made her shiver. "But do you think we could dispense with this bloody coat?"

"It's not that bad," she said, fighting a grin. "My grandmother gave it to me."

"Well, she didn't do you any favors," Ian commented as he helped her out of the sleeves. He took the garment and dumped it on the couch, glad to finally be rid of the ugly thing. Trust Jillie to take in stray coats as well as stray cats, he thought as he turned back—and momentarily forgot how to breathe.

She stood near the window, moonlight pouring over her like a silver river. She seemed made of light, a gossamer dream spun of night and magic, a fantasy come to life. And yet she was real, so very real. In the cab he'd had a taste of what loving her would be like —a sweet slice of heaven melting through his frozen soul. One taste would never be enough. "Jillie," he said softly, half afraid she'd vanish like so many of his other dreams, "you can dispense with the dress as well."

She went utterly still. For a moment he thought he'd pushed her too far too fast—this was so new for both of them. Then she reached behind her and slid down the zipper. For a moment she held the bodice of the soft material like a shield against her chest. Then with a barely audible sigh she loosened her death grip on the velvet darkness and let it fall to her ankles.

She was a vision. Her high, smallish breasts were fuller than he'd imagined, with dark, straining nipples that seemed to beg for his touch. Her torso narrowed to an impossibly small waist, then flared again to generous hips that called up a hundred carnal images to mind. His gaze traveled down and up her slim legs, to the black lace panties that revealed almost as much as they concealed. She had the figure of a courtesan, not a cybertech, and her unconsciously erotic sensuality brought him to instant, aching arousal. "Ms. Polanski," he said roughly as he fought to control his fierce, primal need, "my simulator did *not* do you justice."

He started to pull off his sweater, but her soft words stopped him.

"No. Let me."

She walked over to him, trying not to look as eager as she felt. She wanted to touch him so badly, it made her weak, but what if she did it wrong? She knew her love could meet his emotional needs, but his physical ones . . . she was less certain. She reached him and bunched the bottom of his sweater in her hands, shocked at how the feel of the soft, Ian-warm material ignited her own desire. Instinctively she raised the cloth to her face and rubbed it against her cheek.

He uttered a sharp, raw curse. "Take it off," he commanded hoarsely. "Now."

Obeying, she pulled the sweater over his head, but when she tried to discard it she found he'd looped the material around the back of her neck and was pulling her to him. "You get me crazier than any woman on earth," he said as he placed slow, tantalizing kisses at the edges of her mouth. "Why is that?"

*Because I love you.* But she wasn't brave enough to say it, not yet. "We've spent a lot of time in the simulator. Maybe it's the fantasy you fell for, not me."

"Lord, is that what you think?" He dropped the sweater and folded her in his arms, hugging her fiercely. "Do you know why I'm so at home in cyberspace? It's because I've spent my whole life in virtual realities. I grew up in that god-awful castle with a grandfather who was so busy living up to the expectations of the dead that he had no time for the living. I married a woman who wanted me to play the high-profile, jet-setting aristocrat, who left when it became apparent that I wasn't going to give up my scientific studies for her caviar dreams.

"And now I'm *Dr. Doom*," he chuckled, though there was no humor in his tone. "I'm the forbidding, steel-skinned scientist with a calculator for a heart."

"You're not steel-skinned," she offered huskily, her response muffled against his naked chest.

"Only to you," he murmured, placing a reverent kiss against her temple. "You have a way about you—

of drawing the best out of people whether they want you to or not." He lifted his head, looking at the mishmash of ecology memorabilia on her living room walls. "I suppose it's because you care so damn much about this world and all the creatures in it. And for some unfathomable, blessed reason, you've chosen to care about me."

"I don't think choice had much to do with it," she confessed shakily. Her passion for him consumed her on every level—emotional, spiritual, physical . . . very, very physical. His hands stroked fire along her skin, kneading the sensitive flesh of her breasts and buttocks, making her hot and tight in places she didn't even know she had. Moaning, she buried her face in the softness of his chest, wild for the smell and taste of him, wild for much more. He was driving her full tilt toward the edge of passion, but she couldn't allow herself to fall into it, not just yet. "There's something I need to tell you."

"I'm all ears," he murmured, though his next X-rated move proved that parts of him were *definitely* not ears.

"Ian, stop . . . Ian!" she cried, torn between delight and frustration. Summoning the last vestige of her willpower, she pushed herself away from the honeyed fire of his hands, holding herself at arm's length. "I need to tell you something. Something important."

"Something quick, I hope," he commented, staring shamelessly at her breasts.

Incorrigible, that's what he was. And she loved

him all the more for it. "Ian, there's no way to say this except right out. I . . . I don't have a father."

"All right, you don't have a father. Let's get back to—"

"Ian, you're not listening!" She turned away and went to the window, looking out over the ocean as she confessed the damning truth. "My mother wasn't married to my father. Hell, she didn't even know who he was. She told me once that the best she could do was narrow it down to three people . . . unless it was this bouncer in Omaha who gave her a ride on his motorcycle. Anyway, you get the picture. Mom wasn't exactly discriminating when it came to men, and she made a lot of mistakes. I'm the mistake she had to live with."

Ian said nothing. How could he? There was nothing to say. He was a baron, and she was the result of a moment's indiscretion. "It makes a difference, doesn't it?" she said, her voice heavy with misery.

In two strides he reached her and turned her around, grasping her by the shoulders, giving her a slight but distinct shake of frustration. "Listen, I'm not sure what you expected this bit of information would mean to me, but I must tell you that I couldn't care less about your background or your parents."

"It doesn't matter to you?" she said softly.

"*You* matter to me," he stated passionately. "And if I hadn't been such a blockhead, I'd have told you this afternoon, when that Nazi bastard pointed his gun at your heart. I'd have taken my bloody machine apart bolt by bolt if anything had happened to—"

He got no further. She threw her arms around his neck and stopped his mouth with a soul-demolishing kiss. It was the kind of passion he'd thought existed only in stories, dreams, and the fantasy world of the simulator. But the woman in his arms was real. The lush mouth laving hot, hungry caresses on his was real. The words of love and promise she whispered in his ear were real.

"Tell me I'm not in the simulator," he breathed as he buried his face in the fragrant silk of her hair.

"You're not in the simulator," she assured him, trailing sweet kisses down the side of his neck.

He ran his hands down the long, bare length of her back, groaning with pleasure. "Tell me I'm not dreaming."

"You're not dreaming," she said as she began to attack his belt. "Any more questions, Doctor?"

"Just one," he replied with a devilish grin. "Where's your purse?"

The adventure that followed put every one of the simulator's alternate realities to shame. Beneath Ian's sober surface lurked an unexpected vein of pure mischief, and soon Jill found herself almost as breathless from laughter as she was from his searing caresses. The search for her purse quickly morphed into a contest to see which of them could remove the other's clothing in the most original manner. Initially Jill had more opportunity, since Ian was wearing more clothes than she was, but when Ian removed her panties with his teeth, even she had to declare him the winner.

Naked, their games became more serious and their laughter more rough-edged. The mutual passion they'd spent months denying came out in white-hot fury. They started up the stairs to Jill's bedroom, but made it only as far as the landing. Ian buried his fingers in her hair and plundered her mouth again and again, feeding on her like a starving man at a feast. Then he moved to claim other areas of her anatomy—an ear, her throat, and finally her breasts. He gorged himself on her, sucking her sweet ripeness until she cried aloud with pleasure. Then he covered her mouth with his again, and claimed the sound of her passion too.

Jill writhed against him, glorying in the carnal magic of his kiss. Blazing light and heat seared into the lost places deep inside her soul. She wallowed in the pleasure of smelling and tasting his skin, of discovering the rough, salty, sensual textures of the man she loved. He was beyond fantasy. With love-blurred vision she lifted her head and gazed past his shoulder at the half-dozen steps that separated the landing from the upstairs hallway. "Doctor," she confessed hoarsely, "I don't think we're going to make it to my bedroom."

He laughed deeply, and pressed a smoldering kiss into the shadowed valley between her breasts. "Ms. Polanski, I can guarantee we won't."

The games were over. They dropped to their knees on the landing, wrapped in each other's arms and passion. They roamed kisses over each other's face and shoulders, as if they still couldn't believe that this was real. Ian's hand found her swollen breast and roughly kneaded her into a frenzy, his iron control finally succumbing to the holocaust force of his desire. Leaning back, he grasped her waist and pulled her up to straddle his lap. His hardness jabbed into the soft skin of her inner thigh, making her go absolutely still. For a moment they stared at each other, silent except for the tortured sound of their breathing. "Jillie," he rasped, "you're so small. I don't want to hurt—"

His words ended in a ragged gasp as she moved over him and impaled herself on his erection.

"Bloody hell!" he cursed as she fell against his chest, shuddering. "Jill, I don't want—"

"I want," she breathed softly. "Don't make me wait, Ian. Let me love you . . ."

Then her inner contractions took over, seducing him deeper into her body, loving him in ways that blasted every fantasy he'd ever had into oblivion. Leaving her was no longer an option. He moved within her, setting up the rhythm he'd started on their first trip into the simulator, when he'd saved her from the orc. Illusion became reality as she locked her slim legs around his hips and joined him in the ancient dance of love. *Love.* He slid his hand between their bodies, stroking her soft curls as he increased the strength of his thrusts. She clung to him, crying his name as he brought her to a swift, sweet climax. He wanted to savor her pleasure, but his own desire seized him in a fiery grip. Driving into her, he at last took his own release, destroyed and remade in the furnace of their love.

Spent beyond measure, he leaned back against the wall, knowing that she'd given him back a part of himself he'd thought lost forever—his belief. "I thought dreams couldn't come true," he said with a short, gasping laugh. "I was wrong."

She lay against his chest, her face hidden from view. But between her soft, rapid breaths he felt her lips pull into a smile. "There's always a first time, Doctor. Care to try for a second?"

Ian hooked his thumb in his jeans' waistband and eyed the interior of Jill's refrigerator with a frown of dismay. "Don't you have any *real* food?"

Jill's eyes and nose appeared over the top of the refrigerator door. "What do you mean? There's lots of food in there."

"Yes, if I were a rabbit." He picked up a container of bean sprouts and gave its contents a suspicious sniff. "Good Lord, even your bloody cat gets a hearty breakfast," he said, glancing over to where Merlin was industriously devouring a can of cat food. "Don't you have any eggs, or bacon?"

"Cholesterol and nitrates? I don't think so." She came around the door and ducked under his arm. Pulling her oversize Save the Manatee T-shirt close against the sudden cold, she bent down and examined the health-food-stuffed shelves. "However, if you've really got your heart set on something seminutritious, I think I've got some—hey!"

Ian's arms shot out and circled her middle, pulling her against his bare chest, still damp from his recent shower. "I think I've found what I want for breakfast," he growled as he nuzzled her ear.

"Ian, stop it!" she cried, trying to sound affronted. It was an impossible task. Her heart was too full of the love they'd shared the night before, the glorious hours they'd spent finding joy and acceptance in each other's arms.

After their first frantic encounter on the stairs, they'd donned their clothes and driven to an all-night drugstore, where Ian had purchased a new box of condoms. They'd made it back to the garage before they'd made love again—this time indulging in raw, hot sex in the backseat of her car. Afterward they'd lain in each other's arms, savoring the golden afterglow of their love.

At three they finally made it to her bedroom. Ian fell asleep almost immediately, but Jill lay awake for almost an hour, simply listening to the sound of his deep, measured breathing. She savored every minute of their passionate lovemaking, but lying next to him in the dark filled her with a peace she'd never known.

All her life she'd felt ashamed of her birth—the unwanted, embarrassing result of a purely physical coupling. But Ian's pragmatic acceptance of her past made her see it in a whole new light. A respectable heritage wasn't any guarantee of happiness. His privileged, pedigreed background had brought him nothing but a lonely childhood and a social-climbing wife. Because of Ian she realized it wasn't so much how a person started out in this life that mattered, it was where they ended up. And she thanked She took a stiff gulp of her drink, but even its fire couldn't cut the funeral chill building inside her.God she was lucky enough to end up in Ian's arms.

However, there was a time and place for everything.

"Ian," she said, trying again, "much as I'd like to be your 'breakfast,' we don't have the time. We've got to get to the simulator lab and set up the cyberspace environment so we can find Einstein."

"Not this time. Jill, I've decided to go in alone."

"But you need a cyberpartner," she said, stunned. "It's the rule."

"Yes, but I *make* the rules. Einstein is in danger, and anyone who goes after him will be in danger too. I've decided the risk is too great to jeopardize more than one life. I'm going in alone."

"Like hell you are. I'm coming with you whether you like it or—"

Her sentence ended in a startled gasp as Ian's hands delved between her thighs and began caressing her through the soft cotton of her T-shirt. His bold, possessive strokes took her apart in a matter of seconds, and she arched back against him, giving a whimper of pleasure. "You're trying to distract me," she accused him.

His warm chuckle teased her ear. "Is it working?"

She nodded weakly. Moaning, she reached up and circled the corded muscles at the back of his neck, and guided his mouth down to hers for a deep, wanton kiss. When he finally lifted his head, he was just as breathless as she was. Smiling triumphantly, she added, "It's working, but I'm still not letting you go into the simulator alone."

"Hell, Jillie." Ian untangled their bodies and plowed his hand through his hair, riveting her with a stare cold enough to freeze water. "I forbid it."

Jill crossed her arms and shot him back a look every bit as cool as his. "I don't care."

"Argh!" he cried, throwing up his hands. He stalked out of the kitchen and into the living room, heading for the plate-glass window that looked out over the ocean. The sun had just crested the horizon, streaming a pure and sacred light over the face of the waters. Through the half-open door he smelled the fresh salt of the sea breeze, and heard the hushed and peaceful sound of the breaking waves. But there was no peace in his heart.

Damn the woman! Couldn't she see he was just trying to protect her? His mind wandered back to the tales he'd read of his medieval ancestors who'd ridden off to the Crusades with King Richard. Several of them had locked their wives up in towers during their absence. Ian rubbed his chin, thinking that what had once seemed like a cruelty now sounded like a very sensible precaution.

He wasn't used to being disagreed with. But then, he also wasn't used to waking up with Jillie's soft body spooned against his, or having her kiss him awake with a dozen butterfly caresses. For the first time in longer than he could remember he was looking forward to the day ahead, instead of merely enduring it. Perhaps a disagreement or two could be forgiven.

"Ian."

She came up behind him and circled his chest with her arms, pressing herself against his bare back. He closed his eyes, savoring the intoxicating feel of her, blessing and cursing the love he felt for this sweet, irresistible, and frustratingly independent woman.

"Ian, do you know why I left your company?"

"No," he said truthfully. "I assumed Sheffield made you a better offer."

"That wasn't it. The money was the same, but I would have gone even if meant taking a pay cut. I couldn't stay in your company. I couldn't stand watching you go into the simulator, knowing that you might never come out again."

"Jill—"

"No, let me finish," she said, hugging him tighter. "You don't know what it was like. I felt as if someone were squeezing my heart every time you stepped into the egg. I couldn't take it."

He covered her hands with his. "I thought you couldn't stand me."

"I couldn't stand the way you made me feel. And I was mad as hell at you for never letting anyone else get close to you, and taking the risks you did." She paused, breathing a deep, ragged sigh. "I guess I still am."

He lifted one of her hands and placed a lingering kiss in the center of her open palm. "Nothing's going to happen to me."

"But if it did . . ." She loosened her hold and came around to stand in front of him, looking up at him with her huge, impossibly lovely eyes. "Don't you see?" she said in a hushed, tight voice. "If something were to happen to you, I'd want it to happen to me too."

"Jillie." He wrapped his arms around her and hugged her hard, wishing he didn't know exactly how she felt. He couldn't imagine living without her either. "Right, then," he said with his trademark harrumph. "This afternoon we'll go into the simulator together. But at the first sign of trouble, I'm sending you out, no matter what you . . . Ms. Polanski, what do you think are you doing?"

"Distracting you," she said sweetly, using much the same method that he had. "Is it working?"

"You bloody well know it is," he answered. The lady was dynamite. Without warning he swung her into his arms and tumbled her onto the couch. "And I still haven't had my breakfast."

"Ian, we can't," she said, caught between laughter and alarm. "It's broad daylight, and the windows are wide open. The neighbors will think I'm marrying a sex maniac."

He stilled in her arms. "What did you say?"

"I said sex maniac, my love. Not that I mind, but —Ian, what's wrong?"

He pulled away and sat heavily on the cushion beside her. "Jill, I thought you understood. What we have is wonderful, but there are no guarantees that it will last. Just being together for now should be enough."

# THIRTEEN

Nothing had changed. The sunlight streaming through the sliding glass door was just as brilliant as it had been a moment before. The clock on the mantel still ticked out its measured minutes. Nothing had changed—and yet, everything had changed. Suddenly Jill felt as if she were in the simulator, transported into a digital copy of her living room, a sham of reality. The rules were different here. Two and two made five in this world. Two hearts added up to zero. And the man whose love had seemed as reliable as the force of gravity had become a stranger wearing Ian's face.

Loving and being loved by Ian had completed her in ways she couldn't begin to fathom, filling up the empty places inside her with laughter and love. But apparently that love had been only an illusion, like a magician's carnival trick. Ian was still the titled lord of the manor. She was still the unforeseen result of a brief and meaningless affair. "I see."

"No, you don't see. I can tell by your voice that you don't." Ian rose to his feet and started to pace the rug, his fierce steps betraying his frustration. "It's got nothing to do with you—it has to do with love itself. It's just not realistic to assume that two completely separate and distinct individuals will spend the rest of their lives together. The statistics bear me out—one out of two marriages end in divorce."

"And one out of two doesn't," she offered quietly.

"Well—harrumph—that's true, but it's still an unacceptable percentage. No intelligent scientist would enter into an experiment with that kind of success rate. Marriage in today's society is—" He halted before the sliding glass door, running his hand through his thick, damp hair as he searched for the right words. "Marriage is just not logical."

*Logical.* The scientific word lashed her like a whip. She looked up, searching Ian's profile for a trace of the man she loved. But all she found were the cold, remote features of the emotionless Dr. Doom.

"Truthfully, it's a miracle when two people do stay together," he continued. "And I don't believe in miracles."

Jill closed her eyes, hearing her mother's voice.

*Promise me*, her mother whispered.

She shivered, feeling the chilling hand of reality push away her golden dream. Too clearly she recalled what "logical" relationships had done to her mother's life. *Never settle for half of a man's love.*

Opening her eyes, Jill glanced at Ian's severe profile. Even now she sensed the ache inside him, conscious of the wonderful, terrible awareness that linked her to him in ways she couldn't understand. She knew she'd love this outwardly stern, inwardly gentle man until the day she died. She also knew that it didn't make a bit of difference to him.

Slowly she uncurled herself from the couch and rose to her feet. "It's getting late. I guess we'd better get to the lab—"

"Bugger the lab," Ian stated. He swiveled around and strode across the room toward her, his long shadow cutting a dark swatch across the sun-bright carpet. "I want to be certain you understand me."

"Oh, I understand, all right," she said coolly. "You want me to become your mistress."

The word stopped him mid-step. "For God's sake, Jill, it's not like that at all. What I'm offering you is a mature, honest relationship—"

"What you're offering me," she said, raising her chin proudly, "is the same thing all those men offered my mother."

Ian froze. His jaw pulled into a tight, thin line, and his eyes took on their most frosty metallic sheen. His steely gaze collided with her determined brown one, sparking fire. They stood in absolute silence, two diametrically opposed forces, separated by several feet and a light-year of philosophy. The tension sizzled between them.

The doorbell shattered the silence.

"Who the—?" Jill began.

"Rogers," Ian replied tersely. "I called him earlier, when I didn't think you were coming to the lab. But he wasn't supposed to pick me up until—good Lord!" he said, glancing at her mantel clock. "Is it that late?"

He started for the door. Jill watched him go, trying to tell herself that she was glad to see the back of him, but the ache in her heart told another story. Then the ache gave way to panic as she realized that Ian was about to head out of her front door half dressed. Angry and hurt as she was, she couldn't let him show up at the lab like that. The techs would never let him live it down.

"Ian, wait!" she cried, hurrying to catch up with his long-legged strides. "You've at least got to put your sweater on."

"Jillie."

She knew that tone. It melted her resolve like butter. Helplessly she turned toward the kitchen and the garage beyond. "I'll get your sweater. It's in the car," she muttered, beginning to move away.

She didn't get far. Ian moved behind her, circling her with his arms. "Dammit, Jillie," he breathed against her ear, "you're always running away from me."

"I have to. Staying with you would kill me."

"And losing you would kill me." He pulled her close, burying his face in the sensitive curve of her neck. "Talk to me, Jill. That's all I—"

The doorbell rang again.

"Bloody hell." He reluctantly loosened his hold on her and started once more for the door.

"Ian, your sweater!"

He glanced back, flashing her a winning smile. "No need, love. I asked Rogers to bring a change of clothes."

Of course he would, Jill thought bleakly. Dr. Doom was never caught off guard. He planned and plotted all his undertakings in a thorough, *logical* manner. "You're always prepared for everything, aren't you?"

His smile sobered. For an instant his eyes lost their hardness, showing her a glimpse of the real, vulnerable man beneath the confident exterior. "I wasn't prepared for you, Jillie," he stated softly. "You took me completely by surprise."

*Me too*, she thought as she watched him leave.

After he'd gone, she started up the stairs, trying to concentrate on the simulator and her mission to find Einstein. She made it three steps before she sank to the carpeted stair, exhausted. Once her cozy condominium had been a haven where she could escape from her desire for Ian. But after last night there wasn't a square inch of the place that didn't hold his memory. Even these stairs reminded her of the first time he'd made love with her, and claimed her heart in the process. In that instant she'd pledged herself to him, body and soul, forever. She'd thought he felt the same.

"To have and to hold, for as long as it's *conve-*

*nient,*" she said, blinking tears from her eyes. Her mother had been right—less than twelve hours into their affair, and it was already tearing her apart.

Once they found Einstein, she was going to turn in her resignation and get as far away from the doctor and his simulator as possible. It wasn't the smartest career move, but it was the only one she could make. She had to get out now, before his halfway love destroyed every ounce of her integrity. Before his rational arguments and irresistible kisses convinced her to stay.

Before their passion had the opportunity to produce another unwanted child.

Ian fell. He tumbled like a rag doll through the layers of bright and dark, a black backdrop populated by matrixes of light. Weird shapes flashed by—neon trapezoids, laser-etched polygons, squares cut with impossibly intricate patterns of sizzling circuitry. He watched it all with clinical interest, unconcerned with his rapid descent or the strangeness of the kaleidoscope shapes around him. He'd been here before, many times. This was raw cyberspace, the first and most primitive of all the topologies generated by the simulator. It was the only overlay his cybertechs could use for the low-core processor sector that Einstein's equations had pointed to. It was also the most dangerous.

His fall slowed as he approached the light-veined surface of zero core. Still, his landing was less than pleasant. He hit the ground belly-first, with enough force to drive the air from his lungs. "Bloody hell," he cursed, rising to his elbows. "Parker, I told you to fix—"

His breath cut off by the force of another body landing on top of his.

"Ohmigod!" Jill cried as she scrambled off him. "Are you okay?"

"I'll live," he said, omitting the fact that his backside ached like one big bruise. He rolled over and sat up, ignoring his discomfort as he took a quick scan of her bodysuit. To his relief, her suit's wire-thin crimson light-lines—the virtual representation of her life-sustaining node connections to the simulator—were still pulsing with unbroken power.

"Ian!" she whispered urgently as she raised a finger to point at something. "What's that!"

Ian tensed, then relaxed. "It's only a grid bug," he told her, rising to his feet and watching the little crablike creature scuttle away across the neon-scored plane. "They can't hurt you, but there are plenty of things in here that can. I want you to stick to me like a second skin. That's an order from your boss."

He reached down and pulled her effortlessly to her feet, bringing her against him in the process. "It's also a request from your lover," he added, his rough whisper making the words a caress.

"Ian, don't," she pleaded, pressing her palms against his chest. "I can't deal with this now . . . I mean, we've got to concentrate on finding Einstein."

"And I thought I was the practical one," he

grumbled, reluctantly releasing her. "But I intend to continue this discussion as soon as we're back in real space. Understood?"

"Uhm, right," she said without meeting his gaze. "As soon as we're back." Turning, she looked out at the vast cyberplane and its jumble of shifting shapes and ever-changing data arrays, all defined in striking laser light. "Wow, this place looks like an amusement park on a bad hair day. Are you sure we're in the right sector?"

"We are according to the digital information in the data dumps we gleaned from the Casablanca airport. We should be within a hundred yards of— watch out!"

Ian grabbed her and yanked her to his side. He was just in time. A small pink meteor sizzled past Jill's head, close enough to singe her hair. "Good Lord," he cried, "I've never seen anything like that before. Control! What is that thing?"

"We're not sure, Doctor," Felix's voice replied. "It whizzed in from another sector at the speed of sound. We could barely get a fix on it before—look out, it's coming back!"

Ian twisted around, and found the thing barreling straight for them. There was no time to escape. Acting on instinct, he shoved Jill behind him, determined to protect her with the only shield he had— his body. "When this thing hits you, run like hell," he commanded.

"Ian, I don't think—"

"Just do it!" He wanted to say more—so much

more—but there wasn't time. He braced his legs for impact, thinking how absurd the situation was. *I've bested an orc and a Nazi, only to be taken out by a powder-pink fireball—*

The fireball stopped dead a foot from his breastbone.

Startled, Ian staggered back as if the thing had hit him after all. "What the—?"

"That's what I was trying to tell you," Jill said as she came around beside him. "I don't think she's dangerous."

"She?"

"Yes, *she*." Jill swung her gaze to the pulsing pink fireball. "PINK, is that you?"

The fireball pulsed brighter.

"The prototype." Ian rubbed his aching temple, coming to grips with the astonishing fact that he and Jill were going to live. "Well, she certainly knows how to make an entrance."

"An entrance she wasn't supposed to make," Jill said, looking disapprovingly at the suspended fireball. "PINK, you know you shouldn't be in here. It's dangerous. I want you to go back this instant."

PINK didn't budge.

"I mean it," Jill continued. "I want you out of here right—" She stopped, distracted by Ian's deep chuckle.

"Looks like there's more than one disobedient female in this cyberplane," he observed with a decidedly unscientific smile. "Anyway, as long as she's here, she might be able to help us locate Einstein."

PINK blazed nova bright. She took off like a rocket toward a large yellow-veined obelisk, then halted and backtracked a few feet. Then she was off again, disappearing from their view, only to reappear, pulsing impatiently.

"I suppose we'd better follow," Ian said, taking a step in PINK's direction. "Remember, stay close. I'm not entirely certain what's out there. But whatever it is," he added as he took the hand of the woman beside him, "we'll face it together."

*For now, anyway*, Jill thought bleakly.

She'd lied to Ian. He expected to take up where they left off as soon as they left the simulator. She hadn't told him that she'd already faxed her resignation to the human resources department at Sheffield and had deposited a copy on his desk just before she'd gone to the lab. When she left the simulator this time she intended to keep right on walking, leaving the company and Ian behind for good.

She'd done the right thing—the only thing she could do considering the situation. But as she walked beside him in this uncharted topology, his strong hand clasping hers, facing danger as his partner, she felt more miserable than she'd thought possible. Every step she took in this virtual reality meant a step closer to the end of their mission—and the end of their love in the real world. *The nearer we get to finding PINK's love, the nearer I get to losing mine. . . .*

The terrain changed. Mammoth shapes rose up around them in scattered, broken chunks, like the remains of city buildings after an earthquake. Light lines snaked and hissed like severed power lines, and the air was full of the throat-scarring smells of smoke and ash. The temperature rose, making Jill feel hot and uncomfortably sticky in her skin-tight bodysuit. "Can't we have Felix whip up an iceberg or something?"

"Jillian," Ian sighed, "one doesn't just 'whip up' something in cyberspace. Topology generation is an intricate and exacting science. Physical laws have to be adhered to, just as they are in the real world."

"I guess there's no law about neatness," she said, glancing at the devastation around her. Despite the heat, a cold chill shivered up her back. *Someone just walked over my grave.*

As they walked on, the landscape became even more perilous. Toppled shapes lay across their path, boulders crisscrossed with sputtering, fading light. PINK flew past the obstacles, but Jill and Ian had to climb over the rubble, slipping and skidding on the loose, treacherous talus. Wide fissures opened in the ground, and more than once Ian's anchoring grasp saved Jill from plunging into one of the dark pits.

Finally, they reached what appeared to be a stable plateau. Jill sank down against a broken half-sphere, exhausted beyond words. Ian was just as winded, but instead of resting he knelt beside what appeared to be a severed cobalt-blue power grid line.

"This shouldn't have happened," he muttered as he stared at the cut grid line. "The simulator matrix is supposed to prevent this kind of disintegration. It goes against every law of cyberphysics. It's not . . . logical."

Jill was quickly growing to hate that word. "Well, logical or not, it's happening. Apparently someone's taken 'raping the environment' into the virtual plane."

"It's more than that. Someone's warping the fabric of cyberspace itself. Someone . . . or something."

Ian stood up, his tall form towering over the broken shapes on the plateau. Jill couldn't take her eyes off him. Against the black backdrop, the crimson lines of his bodysuit pulsed like hellfire. *He's part of this world,* she thought as she watched him move confidently through the weird landscape. *A sorcerer in his magic realm.* Once again a shiver crept up Jill's spine, but this time for the man, not the environment. "What do you mean by 'something'?"

"I'm not sure," Ian said, shooting his silver gaze back at her. "But I am sure that you're leaving. Now."

"Not unless you are," she answered as she got to her feet and raised her chin defiantly. "And if I have to step into one of those stupid blue lines again to stay, I will."

"Dammit, Jill." He strode over to her and grasped her by the shoulders. "This isn't a game. This isn't even an experiment anymore. Something very evil is going on in here, and I've got to find out what it is."

"We've got to—"

"No," he said with devastating softness. "Not this time."

She tried to pull away, but his firm grip prevented it. Too late she realized he'd trapped her, preventing her from moving into one of the nearby lines. "This isn't fair," she cried as she struggled against his hold.

"Yes, well, we'll argue about ethics later," he said smoothly, turning his gaze heavenward. "Sadie, I want you to—"

"There's not going to be a later," Jill interrupted furiously. "I turned in my resignation."

Ian's whole body went stone still. "You *what*?"

"I'm quitting," she replied, words rushing out of her like wine from an uncorked bottle. Tears pricked her eyes, but whether from frustration or despair she didn't know. "I'm not one of your simulations. You can't order me around. You can't make me do what I don't want to do, even if a part of me wants to do it. . . ." Her words dwindled off, ending in a sob. "I can't take it anymore, Ian. I can't take *you*."

If she'd run a broadsword through his heart, he couldn't have looked more shocked. "Is that what you honestly believe?"

"Yes. No," she said, the pain in his eyes tearing her apart. Suddenly Einstein, the voyeuristic cybertechs, even the bizarre world around them, ceased to matter. She lifted her hand to his cheek, caressing him with a bittersweet tenderness. "I love you, but I can't be with you. If I stayed, I know I'd give in to you on everything—and it would eventually destroy me. I'd be going against everything I believed in, and . . . and if we ever made a child—"

Ian's grip tightened almost painfully. "I would never allow that to happen to you."

"Darling, there are some things even you can't guarantee," she replied, smiling sadly. "I can't live without a commitment, and you can't live with one. It's better if I leave. It's . . . it's the only *logical* solution."

Emotions burned in his eyes, but Jill couldn't read the nuances in his virtually synthesized features. He started to speak, but at that moment PINK began buzzing around them like a miniature comet. She made several passes before flying over to a nearby pile of rubble and beginning her circuit all over again.

"She must want us over there," Jill said, welcoming the distraction from her own troubles. "Perhaps there's something in the pile that will lead us to Einstein."

She started to move, but Ian held her back. "Jill," he said quietly, his gaze riveted on the heap, "that's no ordinary pile of rubble."

As he spoke, a thin black layer peeled off the top of the pile and flew off with an inhuman grace of an undersea manta ray. Jill stiffened, revolted by the strange creature in a way that defied logic. It was as if someone had taken her worst dreams and rolled them into one chilling nightmare. "What is that thing?"

"I'm not sure, but it doesn't appear to be alone,"

Ian replied, nodding to the rubble. "The pile's swarming with them."

He was right. Looking closely, Jill saw the surface of the pile undulate as the black sheet creatures moved in and around each other. She shivered, this time in real fear. She wanted to run, to get as far away from the chillingly weird beings as possible. But one thing made it impossible for her to leave. When one of the sheet creatures moved, she saw a spark of blue beneath the black layer. A pulsing blue, beating in perfect unison with PINK's burning globe.

Apparently Ian's thoughts mirrored her own. "Jillie," he said quietly, "I'm afraid we've finally found your Einstein."

# FOURTEEN

Ian froze, feeling as though he'd been catapulted back into one of his childhood nightmares. The gloomy, cavernous corridors of his ancient castle filled his young subconscious with a battalion of monstrosities—from cannibal ghosts and headless ghouls, to a purple-tongued bogeyman with glowing eyes who lived in the shadows under his bed. Science and maturity had overcome these childhood beliefs, but there was still a small, secret part of him that remembered the monsters and recalled the soul-numbing terror felt by a lonely, imaginative boy in the dark hours of the night.

But this was no nightmare. Despite the simulated topology, this danger was very, very real. Ignoring the knot of fear in his stomach, he took a few steps in the direction of the pile. "Get a reading on this, Sadie. The things look like some kind of stray data strings or rogue viruses, but I've never seen them swarm in a community before. I'm going to try to touch one—"

"No!" Jill cried, grasping his arm to hold him back. "Those things are feeding on Einstein. What if they feed on you too?"

"I'm a much weaker energy source. I doubt they'll be interested," he assured her as he removed her hand, holding it a bit longer than was absolutely necessary. *A child. Good Lord, why hadn't he considered what the possibility of having an illegitimate child would do to her?*

Well, there was no time to consider it now. He approached the pile with a hunter's caution, grateful for once for his sportsman grandfather's meticulously drilled instructions. *Never take your eyes off your prey. Never show fear. They can smell it.* He lifted his boot and gave one of the creatures a small shove. The thing didn't even turn in his direction, but merely reshifted to its former position.

Encouraged, he reached down and gripped one, pulling it off the pile. Its slick, undulating surface sent out a strange vibration that repulsed him to the point of nausea, but he held it firm, and threw it with all his strength into the distance. The creature flapped off in the direction he'd thrown it. Apparently its intelligence was limited—it made no attempt to return to the food source.

Once again Ian lifted his eyes to the heavens. "Control, how much time have I got left?"

"Twenty minutes," Sadie's voice returned.

*Only twenty minutes,* he thought, grimly surveying

the large number of creatures covering Einstein. There were dozens. He couldn't remove them all in that short a time.

A shuffle at his side alerted him. He glanced down and saw Jill kneeling beside him, pulling at one of the creatures. The look on her face told him she found them just as vile as he did.

"You'll need help," she said simply.

"Jill, get away from there," he ordered, appalled at having her so close to the nightmare creatures. "These things could be capable of all sorts of unpredictable mutations. You have to toss them away hard enough to set them on a new trajectory, to prevent them from returning. And we don't know if or when one might morph into something that prefers human energy to electronic. It's too dangerous. It's—"

"Save it for someone who cares, Doctor," she stated, gripping the edge of another creature. "I'm staying. Now, are you going to stand around wasting precious time, or are you going to help me get this computer equivalent of toxic waste off E?"

Put that way, he had little choice.

They worked together, peeling off the layers of noxious creatures from Einstein. Twice Jill had to stop, nearly gagging on the revolting smell and feel of the unholy things. She wiped her hands on her bodysuit, wondering if she'd ever be clean again. Only PINK's continual worried buzz kept her reaching back for more. Only PINK's buzz, and Ian's incredible dedication to the task.

The scientist never faltered from his objective,

removing the monstrosities with an almost machine-like dedication. But Jill saw the waves of nausea that crossed his face. *He hates these loathsome things as much as I do, maybe more.*

"I would take care of it," he said suddenly.

"Take care of what?"

"Our child, if we had one. I'd make sure he—or she—was supported financially and emotionally." He rested a scant second, whipping his sweating brow with the back of his arm. "I wouldn't turn my back on our child—or you."

He was trying to be kind, she knew that. But all he managed to do was twist the knife deeper into her heart. "Ian, children need more than financial and emotional support. They need security. They need to know that the people who love them will be there for them—and for each other. They need . . . a loving family."

"Marriage is no guarantee of that," he told her curtly.

"No," she agreed, "but *not* marrying is almost a guarantee against it."

He started to say something, but he never got the words out. A sudden wave of nausea rocked him, causing him to lose his balance and crumble to the ground.

"Ian!" Jill was at his side in an instant. She pushed and pulled him over to the side of a nearby rectangle. He leaned back against the surface and closed his eyes, clearly exhausted. "You've got to rest. These things are affecting you much more than they are me."

"No, can't give up—"

"You not only can, you will," she said sternly. "That's an order, Doctor."

He started to argue, but stopped as his practical side got the better of him. "All right," he agreed as his mouth curved into a reluctant smile. "And next time I'm letting *you* take on the orc."

Jill turned away before he could see the wince of pain cross her face. *There's not going to be a next time.*

She scrambled back to the pile and began yanking off the creatures with a vengeance. She was making a difference. Before long she could see Einstein's form clearly between the remaining layers of creatures. Apparently, before he'd been attacked, he'd rearranged his data bytes into a human pattern, perhaps believing that his uncomputerlike shape would drive the things off. But if that had been his plan, it had backfired. The creatures had attacked him anyway, draining him of his electronic power, like vampire bats sucking blood. He lay facedown on the ground, his blue and gold diagonally striped skin fading to a sickly pallor. Even his faint energy pulse had stopped beating.

"Einstein!" she said as she shook his shoulder. "Get up!"

No response.

She shook harder. "We've pulled these damn things off you. We've saved you. Now do your bit and get up!"

"Jill." Ian knelt beside her and reached out, gently extracting her hands from their death grip on Einstein. "I don't think that's going to work."

"Of course it will. He's just unconscious."

"He's more than unconscious," Ian told her, his tone gentle in a way she'd never heard before. He stared at her hands, rubbing his thumbs gently along the back of her fingers. "I know you cared for him, but . . . sometimes you can't make things right, no matter how hard you want to."

Jill stiffened, pulling her hands from his grasp. "You think he's dead. Well, you're wrong. He's in there somewhere. I can feel it."

"His electronic resonance might exist, like the brainwave patterns in a coma patient, but that's all. They've drained him dry. He's gone, Jillie. You'll have to accept it."

Accept it. She'd been accepting things all her life. She'd lived with the fact that her mother never cared deeply for anyone besides herself. She dealt with the reality that her mother's boyfriends never wanted or returned the love her childish heart offered. She understood that Ian's love was not the kind she could build a future on. *Deal with it*, she'd always told herself. *Swallow your disappointment and move on.*

But not this time.

"Help me, Ian. I can't do it alone."

She watched his eyes. Even in his virtual representation she could see his internal battle, the logical scientist struggling with the compassionate man. He pushed his hand through his hair, the static electricity in the simulated environment making his fingers spark with living fire. "Jillie, I—"

He paused, his attention suddenly captured by something to Jill's left. She turned to follow the direction of his gaze, and saw that PINK had left her position of safety several yards off and was hovering close to Einstein's head. "PINK, get back! The creatures are still . . ."

Her words of warning died on her tongue. PINK's fireball flared like a supernova, becoming so bright Jill had to hold up her hand to shield her eyes. "What the—?"

"She's morphing," Ian said, his voice hushed with awe. "She's reconfiguring her simulated pattern within the locked topology. Theoretically I knew it could happen, but—it requires so much directed energy, so much willpower."

Miracle or not, Jill was stunned by PINK's transformation. As she watched, the fireball stretched and expanded, swirling like a miniature whirlwind. Gradually the whirlwind solidified into a humanlike body, a slight, elfin woman with close-cropped black hair and skin cut with pink and silver stripes. Formed a few inches above the ground, she drifted down and knelt beside E's lifeless torso. She placed her hands on his shoulders, just as Jill had done. But, instead of shaking him, she began to pulse with power.

"PINK," Jill whispered, unsure of how to speak to the mythical being in front of her.

PINK raised her head and met Jill's gaze. Her eyes radiated pure light, like the heart of a nuclear reactor, or a star. She said nothing aloud, yet Jill felt PINK's message burn in her mind. *My world. My task.* And, after the echo of those words had died, *my love.*

Ian must have heard PINK too, because he and Jill rose to their feet as one. They backed away, watching as PINK poured her own power into Einstein, bringing him back to life. It was a testament to a love that defied boundaries, that was strong enough to overcome the cessation of electronic impulses, that meant death in any reality. "She shouldn't be able to do that," Ian muttered, his gaze riveted on the pair. "It's not possible."

*Anything's possible with love,* Jill thought. She tried to say the words to Ian, but she couldn't get her mouth to move properly. She was beginning to lose touch with this reality, even though their "time limit" in the simulator was not yet up. Apparently either her intense "physical" exertion, or her prolonged contact with the ray creatures, had speeded up her degradation process. She focused what was left of her concentration and painstakingly raised her hand to tug on the doctor's sleeve. "Ian—"

She froze. Past his shoulder she saw one of the largest of the nightmare creatures gliding steadily toward his unprotected head. Even in her befuddled state she couldn't miss its deadly intent. *At any moment one might morph into something that prefers human energy to electronic. . . .*

She couldn't warn him, so she did the next best thing. She screamed at the top of her lungs and gave him a mighty shove, toppling herself backward in the process. Her scream alerted Felix and Sadie to the danger. They immediately started the exiting procedures. Smiling with relief, she saw the evil creature glide through Ian's fading body.

A sharp crackle and the smell of sulphur alerted her to a new danger. She looked to the side, seeing too late that she'd fallen into the path of the cobalt-blue grid lines, which was already beginning to power up for their exit.

"Jill!" She turned at the faint cry, and saw Ian's ghostly form trying to reach her. Halfway between the two realities he saw her danger, but was powerless to save her. She saw the terror in his expression, but felt none for herself. *He's safe*, she thought, knowing that was all that mattered to her—all that would ever matter. *Looks like I saved you after all, Doctor.*

And then the full power of the simulator blasted through her, and she remembered nothing more.

". . . done everything we could to revive her," Dr. Hassam, head of the coma unit, said as he scanned the wide bank of monitors packed into the intensive care unit. "We've exhausted the possibilities."

Ian barely heard him. He stared at the slim, unmoving form in the bed, the physical shell that housed the spirit of the woman he loved. A dozen tubes and wires connected her slight body to the life-sustaining machines. She'd been this way for almost twenty-four hours, and every minute of those hours felt like a stake driven through his heart. "There must be something more you can do," he said hoarsely. "Some drug. Some medical procedure."

"Not in this case," Hassam admitted sadly. "It's as if her mind has lost all connection with her body. Frankly, it's a miracle she's alive at all."

*A miracle*, Ian thought darkly. What kind of bloody miracle left an innocent woman lying in bed like a discarded corn husk? He twisted his fingers around the metal bed rail, wishing like hell he had the strength to rip it apart. She was there because of him, because she'd sacrificed her own safety to push him out of the way of the creature. And, according to Dr. Hassam's expert opinion, there wasn't a thing he could do to help her.

He tightened his grip on the railing. She'd done it to save him. And though she didn't know it, she'd also saved every future cybernaut. Because of what had happened to her, Felix was able to pinpoint the problem with the grid lines, and was reconfiguring them to make them harmless. Jillie's sacrifice had made Ian's simulator safe for everyone, and would bring him international fame.

Fame he would have gladly consigned to the devil if it could have brought her back to him.

All too clearly he remembered their argument in the simulator, when she'd told him she couldn't take being with him anymore. He'd been confident that he could persuade her to stay in one way or another.

But now, as he looked at her silent form, he wondered if she hadn't found a way to leave him after all.

"Dr. Sinclair?"

Ian turned toward the speaker, a young nurse who'd just stuck his head around the hospital room door. "Yes?" Ian sighed, asking out of instinct rather than interest. Partridge's lessons on manners died hard.

"I just got a call from your lab. They asked me to tell you that the prototype was back on-line, and that the bad data had been purged from the system." He paused, giving an apologetic smile. "I'm not sure what that means, but they said you'd find it important."

*They were wrong. I don't give a damn about the system.* He gave a curt nod of thanks, then turned back to the one thing he did give a damn about. *I can't let you go, Jillie. Not like this.* "Maybe we could stimulate her body somehow. Help her mind to relearn the forgotten connections."

"It's worked in other patients," Hassam agreed, "but in my opinion a program like that wouldn't work for her. She's lost too much. It's just not possible."

*It's not possible.* Ian remembered saying much the same words to Jillian in the simulator as he watched PINK transmit her energy to Einstein's lifeless body. In many ways, a human being's electronic physiology was very similar to a computer's. The senses were the input-output ports. The nerve paths were the data-chip circuitry.

His mind fastened on the similarities with his legendary ruthless tenacity. If PINK could revitalize E, there was a chance he could use the same method to revitalize Jillie.

"Does this hospital have a library?" he asked suddenly.

"Well, yes," the startled Dr. Hassam answered. "But I don't see—"

"You will," Ian interrupted brusquely, and he pivoted and headed for the door. "I'm going to read her every bloody book in that library. And when I'm finished, I'll start on the paper, and the *National Enquirer* if that's all that's available. I'm going to stuff her so full of data that she'll wake up out of sheer overload."

"If she can hear you," Dr. Hassam cautioned.

"She'll hear me," Ian stated confidently as he marched out the door. He didn't voice the rest of his thought.

*She'll hear me because she has to.*

# FIFTEEN

He read her magazine articles. He read her newspapers. He read her science journals, paperback romances, and even the racing form. When his eyes stung and his vision blurred, he told her stories of his early years growing up in the castle, of the fabulous wealth and the impoverishing loneliness he'd experienced as a child. When his voice gave out, he called on his friends and his coworkers to take turns at Jill's bedside. Partridge read her extremely bad poetry from the last century. Marsha religiously told her all the latest gossip in the department. Felix gave a lecture on Dungeons and Dragons. Sadie, whose hobby was cooking, brought in all sorts of savory dishes to wave under Jill's nose, trying to stimulate her olfactory sense. Even Einstein and PINK got involved, barraging her with the most comprehensive collection of useless gambling and shopping-channel facts ever compiled.

Ian's bombardment of Jill's senses was constant and unrelenting. It was also apparently ineffective. During the first two weeks, not one flicker of consciousness was recorded by the ever-vigilant monitors. After three weeks, it appeared Jill was actually beginning to lose ground.

On the twenty-second night of her coma, Ian sat alone by her bedside, reading her Dickens's *A Christmas Carol*. The story had always been one of his favorites, but this time he found the imagery of the ghosts and death disturbing. He looked at Jillie's quiet figure, with its tubes and wires and click-clacking breathing device. *Is that what you are, my darling? A ghost?*

Other disturbing images filled his mind. Several days ago Jill's grandparents had arrived from Nebraska. Good, decent folk, they'd been appalled at the thought of their granddaughter's body being kept alive when there was no hope of recovery. Ian had explained his theory and gotten them to agree to let Jill remain on life support. But as the days passed by with no encouraging results, they began to rethink their decision. Today they'd talked to Dr. Hassam about the procedures for medically "pulling the plug." Ian knew that his time was running out.

He sat in the night-quiet hospital, listening to the breathing device separate the silence into discrete, quantifiable sections. All his professional life he'd put his trust in machines, in the measurable and rational laws of reality. Even his simulator, which created alternate realities, was based on those irrefutable laws. But the love he felt for Jill had blasted a heart-shaped hole in those irrefutable laws. Through it he'd caught a glimpse of another reality—a bright world that cast his own safe, careful existence into dull gray shadow. "I can't go back to the way I was," he confessed to her seemingly unhearing form. "And I can't go on without you. Dammit, Jillie, I *need* you."

His throat was raw from talking, yet he continued, speaking words dredged straight from his heart. "I've lived a lie all my life. When I was a boy I was cast in the role of the heir to the Sinclair title. But I wasn't that heir. When I married, I became the sophisticated husband of an international socialite. That wasn't me either. Even my role as scientist is only a part of who I am. I've lived behind masks for so long, I don't know who I am anymore. But when I look into your eyes, I see the man I want to be—the man I could be. With your help."

He bent closer to her immobile features, willing a response. But, as usual, he saw nothing. *What did you expect?* the rational demons of his mind chided him. *By every verifiable measure she's been dead for weeks. Stop making a bloody fool of yourself. Let her go.*

"No," he promised with all the strength left in him. "Never. I'll never let her go." Ignoring every accepted medical procedure, he grasped her shoulders and gave her a firm shake. "You said you felt that Einstein was still alive. Well, I feel that you are. You're in there somewhere, Jillie, and I want you back. I'll storm the pearly gate of heaven itself if that's what it takes. I'm not giving you up, do you here?" He shook her so roughly, he dislodged her wires. "Wake up, dammit. Come back to me!"

What happened during the next seconds happened so fast he could barely make sense of it. Suddenly the room was full of medical personnel swarming over Jillie's form like a hive of angry bees. A brawny orderly pulled Ian off her, but not before he saw one of the nurses begin to extract her breathing tube. "No," he yelled, fighting the orderly with all the strength left in him. "You can't take her off life support. She'll die!"

"She'll die if we don't," the orderly explained as he bodily dragged Ian from the room. "She'll choke if the tube's left in. Her throat's rejecting it."

"Her throat?" Ian muttered, stunned at what the simple words implied. "You mean she's breathing on her own?"

"Looks like it, man," the orderly replied, grinning. Everyone on the hospital staff knew of Ian's crusade to bring Jill back. "She's one in a million. A miracle."

Ian slumped against the wall, exhausted beyond measure. She was going to live. She'd come back to him after all. "You're right," he said, giving the orderly an exhausted smile. "She's a bloody miracle."

There was a knock on Jill's door.

*Okay, don't panic,* she told herself as she glanced in the pocket mirror she'd borrowed from one of the nurses. *So what if you look like you've just been run over by a semi? He loves you. It won't matter to him.*

*But it matters to me.*

The knock sounded again. She sighed, finally acknowledging that thirty minutes' worth of preening wasn't going to make up for three weeks of near-death coma. *Rats*, she thought as she lifted her eyes to face the door. "Come in."

When he first entered the room, she wondered if someone hadn't played a trick on her. Her elegant doctor was gone, switched for a man in a rumpled suit with several days' growth of beard on his chin. Shocked, she said the first thing that came to mind. "You look terrible."

"I see your bout with death hasn't dulled your honesty," he said drolly. Then his stern mouth curved into a smile so tender, it nearly burst her heart. "How are you?"

"Better now," she answered. As if coming out of the coma weren't miraculous enough, her recovery in the past two days had amazed her doctors. Her gaze roamed over Ian.

He looked so endearingly awkward standing by the door, as though he weren't quite sure he was welcome. *British to the core*, she thought with a shake of her head. "Ian, please come closer. I—"

"No—harrumph—I'd better not," he said, plowing his unkept hair in his trademark gesture of frustration. "You're still somewhat frail from your coma, and I . . . well, I just believe it would be more sensible if I stay over here."

"Sensible? Was it sensible for you to waste weeks on me when everyone else had given me up for dead?"

"Jill, you're getting upset—"

"Damn straight I'm getting upset! I busted my buns to break free from that coma and come back to you, and all *you* can think about is being *sensible*. Well, Doctor," she stated as she began to push herself out of her bed, "if you're not coming over here, then I'll just have to—damn!"

Her limited strength gave out and she fell back into her pillows. Ian was beside her in an instant. "Bloody hell," he growled as he cradled her against him. "When are you going to start listening to me?"

"Probably never," she admitted, her words muffled by his shirt. She breathed in his smell, his warmth, his reality, realizing that despite being pronounced medically and physically sound, she hadn't felt truly alive until that moment. *Loving Ian is what makes me real*, she thought, blinking back sudden tears. "Besides, somebody's got to keep you from being *too* sensible."

"Well, you excel at that, Ms. Polanski." He placed a finger under her chin and lifted her gaze to his. "I don't suppose you'd consider taking on the job on a permanent basis? Marriagewise, I mean."

Jill's heart pounded so hard, she thought it would break through her chest. "But you said—"

"I know what I said. And I was a bloody fool for saying it. I spouted off philosophy and high-minded ideals, when the truth was I couldn't bear the thought believing you'd be mine forever, then losing you."

"What made you change your mind?"

"I thought I could control my love for you—box it up like one of my neat equations. But that's not going to be possible. Loving you isn't part of my life, it *is* my life," he confessed, hugging her with a fierce, possessive tenderness. "While you were in the coma I had a glimpse of what my future would be like without you. It is not a reality I would want to live in."

"Are you sure?" she asked, hardly daring to believe the tendrils of rainbows beginning to shine inside her. "Are you absolutely sure?"

"I would estimate the probability to be somewhere around a hundred percent," he said in his most official Dr. Doom voice. "Besides, everyone is counting on it. I mentioned to a few people that we were going to get married, and it took off from there."

"Took off?"

"Like the space shuttle," he acknowledged, grinning. "Partridge is gathering wallpaper samples so you two can redecorate 'the Mausoleum.' Marsha signed herself up for maid of honor. The cybertechs are planning to throw us a 'surprise' engagement party—Sadie promised to give us fair warning. And Einstein—"

"Einstein," a familiar electronic voice interrupted, "is getting sick and tired of listening to all this lovey-dovey stuff."

"E!" Jill cried, turning toward the far corner of the room. She hadn't noticed the unobtrusive gray notebook computer sitting demurely in the shadows —a computer whose screen suddenly blossomed with blue and gold fireworks.

"Hey, babe. What's shakin'?"

Jill laughed at the dear, familiar phrase. "Is it really you? How are you feeling?"

"Fit as a digitally modulated fiddle," Einstein buzzed emphatically. "Thanks to you and the doc here."

"And PINK," Jill added.

"PINK too," E added, his tone dropping to a low resonance Jill had never heard him use before. "I wouldn't be here without her. Of course," he added, his voice resuming its jaunty cadence, "she's not letting me forget it either. Made me run her entire bioanalysis program for edible seaweed products just so she could spend the day handicapping the races at Hialeah. We are talking the Super Bowl of boring. Women!"

Ian chuckled in agreement until Jill thumped him one in the chest. "That was very gentlemanly of you, Einstein."

"Natch. I'm the best there is, there was, there ever will be," he stated without even a pretense of modesty. "Well, Doc, now that Jill's on-line, I guess you'll want some match-merge time. I'm outta here."

"Match-merge?" Ian asked as the computer signed off.

"That's E's expression for romance," Jill explained. "Says it all, don't you think?"

"No. *This* says it all," he said, slanting his mouth over hers. For a long time the only sounds in the room were passionate sighs and the tortured groans of the mattress springs. Finally Ian spoke. "Jillie, you may be up to this, but I'm not," he confessed raggedly as he got up from the bed. "Like your computer friend said, 'I'm outta here.'"

"We've got to invite him to our wedding," Jill stated. "PINK too. We owe them so much."

"Like how to fight for those you love no matter what the conventional wisdom says," Ian agreed, smiling down at her. "I'd like them to be there, but I don't see how."

"You'll figure out something," she said with absolute confidence. "You miraculously brought me back from the dead, didn't you?"

"It's only fair. You brought me back from a living death." He bent down, unable to resist the soft temptation of her loving smile. Straightening at last, he gave her a final, stern appraisal. "You know, Ms. Polanski, you've completely ruined my studies. I never had to bother with miracles before I met you. Now I'll have to factor them into all my equations."

# EPILOGUE

It was one of the most unusual weddings ever to take place in the old, stone-walled Florida garden. The white gazebo and the folding chairs set up for the guests were quite normal, and the large reception tent off to the side was utterly common. But the yards and yards of wires strung like twine through the overhanging branches of the palms and live oaks were not usual in the least. Nor were the dozen video cameras, the oversize satellite dish, the strategically placed microphones, speakers, power relays . . .

"Lawd," Jill's grandfather said as he peered around the edge of the shielding wall toward the gazebo, "there's enough equipment out there to launch a moon rocket."

"Not quite, Pops," she assured him with an indulgent smile. "Ian and his team rigged this up so that the two computer prototypes could attend the ceremony."

"So you said," her grandfather remarked, then shook his head as if to say this would *never* happen in Nebraska. "Is this what you want, Jillie?"

"More than anything," she assured him as she linked her arm through his. Loving and being loved by Ian had soothed all hurting places inside her, making her forget the pain of her early years. But one memory remained, of a mother's final hope for her daughter. *Promise me, Jillie.* "I wish . . . I wish Mom could have been here."

Her grandfather took her hand and gave it a comforting squeeze. "Somehow, I think she is."

Jill started to reply, but stopped as the strains of the "Wedding March" began to fill the air. Marsha stuck her head around the shielding wall. "Hey, guys, it's show time!"

Pops put on his most patriarchal smile and led Jill down the grass aisle past the small assembly. Felix and Sadie nudged each other as she passed, grinning like Cheshire cats, while both Partridge and Jill's grandmother were busy dabbing away tears of happiness. But Jill had eyes only for the tall, midnight-haired man who stood in front of the gazebo, whose gentle smile held more warmth than a thousand suns.

"Hey, look up there!" Felix cried suddenly.

All eyes turned to the sky. Jill gasped in wonder as she saw a brilliant rainbow stretched across the heavens. Astonished, she glanced back at Ian to see what he made of the amazing sight, and caught him winking at her. "You did this? But how—"

"The prototypes helped. We postulated the sun angle, barometric pressure, wind velocity, and so forth. Then we seeded the clouds—and crossed our fingers." His smile deepened as he added, "There's nothing mysterious about water condensation, Ms. Polanski."

*And romance was no excuse for inaccuracy, or so he'd said in Casablanca,* Jill remembered. She took the few final steps to the altar, recalling the seemingly uncrossable distance they'd traveled to get there. She and Ian had come from different worlds, but as she stood beside him, she again felt the potent awareness between them, the unseen power that had drawn their hearts together even while their minds were at odds. "I love you," she whispered.

"I love you," he replied. And then, because part of him would always be her dear, impatient Dr. Doom, he asked the preacher, "I say, can't we just skip to the kissing part?"

Laughter rumbled through the audience. The sound was transmitted through the wires, digitized, and broadcast via the satellite dish to the vast computer complex at Sheffield Industries headquarters. There it was fed into the sensory input ports of the gigantic network CPU, where it was processed by the two wedding guests who couldn't personally attend the ceremony, but who nevertheless absorbed every detail. They sat in adjoining sectors, their bit patterns intertwined as they "watched" Jill and Ian exchange their vows.

PINK gave the digital equivalent of a heartfelt sigh. "Isn't it romantic?"

"I guess," Einstein replied glumly. "But I *still* think it would have been better if they'd listened to me and hired a reggae band."

# THE EDITOR'S CORNER

At this time of year there is always much to be thankful for, not the least of which are the four terrific romances coming your way next month. These stories are full of warmth, passion, and love—just the thing for those cold winter nights. So make a date to snuggle up under a comforter and read the LOVESWEPTs we have in store for you. They're sure to heat up your reading hours with their witty and sensuous tales.

The wonderfully talented Terry Lawrence starts things off with a hero who's **A MAN'S MAN**, LOVESWEPT #718. From the moment Reilly helps Melissa Drummond into the helicopter, she is enthralled—mesmerized by this man of mystery who makes her feel safe and threatened all at once! Sensing the needs she's long denied, he tempts her to taste desire, to risk believing in a love that will last. Once he's warned her that he'll woo her until he's won, she must trust his promises enough to vow her own. This tale of irresistible courtship is another Terry Lawrence treasure.

**THE COP AND THE MOTHER-TO-BE,** LOVESWEPT #719, is the newest heartwarming romance from Charlotte Hughes. Jake Flannery had shared Sammie Webster's grief at losing her husband, cared for her as her child grew inside her, and flirted with her when she knew no one could find a puffy pregnant lady sexy—but she doesn't dare wonder why this tough cop's touch thrills her. And Jake tries not to imagine making love to the feisty mom or playing daddy to her daughter. But somehow their cherished friendship has turned to dangerous desire, and Jake must pull out all the stops to get Sammie to confess she'll adore him forever. The ever popular Charlotte Hughes offers a chance to laugh and cry and fall in love all over again.

Get ready for Lynne Bryant's **DAREDEVIL,** LOVESWEPT #720. Casey Boone is Dare King's buddy, his best friend, the only girl he's ever loved—but now that he might never walk again, Dare King struggles not to let her see his panic . . . or the pain he still feels three years after she left him at the altar! Casey has never stopped loving her proud warrior but fears losing him as she'd lost her dad. Now she must find the courage to heal Dare—body and soul—at last. In this touching and sizzling novel, Lynne Bryant explores the power of love, tested but enduring.

Linda Cajio wants you to meet an **IRRESIST-IBLE STRANGER,** LOVESWEPT #721. Leslie Kloslosky doesn't believe her friend's premonition that she'll meet the perfect man on her vacation in

England—right up to the instant a tall, dark stranger enters the cramped elevator and lights a fire in her blood! Fascinated by the willowy brunette whose eyes turn dark sapphire when he kisses her, Mike Smith isn't about to let her go . . . but will he be clever enough to elude a pair of thieves hot on their trail? Linda Cajio weaves a treasured romantic fantasy you won't forget.

Happy reading!

With warmest wishes,

Beth de Guzman

Senior Editor

P.S. Don't miss the women's novels coming your way in December: **ADAM'S FALL,** from blockbuster author Sandra Brown, is a deliciously sensual story of a woman torn between her duty and her heart; **PURE SIN,** from nationally bestselling author Susan Johnson, is a sensuous tale of thrilling seduction set in nineteenth-century Montana; **ON WINGS OF MAGIC,** by the award-winning Kay Hooper, is a classic contemporary romance of a woman who must make a choice between protecting her heart and surrendering to love once more. We'll be giving you a sneak peek at these wonderful books in next month's LOVESWEPTs. And immediately following this page look for a preview of the terrific romances from Bantam that are *available now!*

Don't miss these incomparable books
by your favorite Bantam authors

On sale in October
*WANTED*
*by Patricia Potter*

*SCANDAL IN*

*SILVER*
*by Sandra Chastain*

*THE WINDFLOWER*
*by Sharon and Tom Curtis*

Winner of the *Romantic Times* 1992
Storyteller of the Year Award

# PATRICIA POTTER

## NATIONALLY BESTSELLING AUTHOR OF *RELENTLESS* AND *NOTORIOUS*

# WANTED

*Texas Ranger Morgan Davis hadn't grown up with much love, but he had been raised with respect for duty and the law. To him, Lorilee Braden was nothing but a con artist, yet her fire and beauty drew him despite his better judgment. Still, her brother was wanted for murder—and the face on the wanted poster looked far too much like Morgan's for comfort. The only way he could clear his own name was to bring Nicholas Braden to justice . . . before the spark Lori had lit became a raging blaze that consumed everything Morgan believed in . . .*

Braden balked at moving again. "Where's my sister?"

"In back," Morgan said. He led his prisoner to the tree several yards behind the cabin. The woman immediately saw Nicholas Braden, her eyes resting on the handcuffs for a moment, then she glared at Morgan.

Braden stepped over to his sister, stooped down,

and awkwardly pulled the gag from her mouth. "Are you all right?"

Morgan leaned back lazily against a tree and watched every movement, every exchange of silent message between the sister and brother. He felt a stab of longing, a regret that he'd never shared that kind of caring or communication with another human being.

Braden tried to untie his sister, but the handcuffs hindered him. Morgan heard a muffled curse and saw the woman's face tense with pain.

"Move away," Morgan said to Braden. Braden hesitated.

"Dammit, I'm not going to keep repeating myself." Irritation and impatience laced Morgan's words.

Braden stood, took a few steps away.

"Farther," Morgan ordered. "Unless you want her to stay there all night."

Braden backed up several feet, and Morgan knelt beside Lorilee Braden. With the knife from his belt, he quickly cut the strips of cloth binding her. Unfamiliar guilt rushed through him as he saw blood on her wrists. He hadn't tied her that tightly, but apparently the cloth had cut into her skin when she'd struggled to free herself.

His gaze met hers, and he was chilled by the contempt there. He put out his hand to help her up, but she refused it, trying to gain footing by herself. Her muscles must have stiffened because she started to fall.

Instinctively reaching out to help her, Morgan dropped the knife, and he saw her go for it. His foot slammed down on it. Then her hand went for the gun in Braden's gunbelt, which Morgan had slung over his shoulder.

Morgan swore as he spun her around, his hand going around her neck to subdue her. Out of the corner of his eye, he saw Nicholas Braden move toward him. "Don't," Morgan said. "I might just make a mistake and hurt her."

All rage and determination, she was quivering against him, defying him with every ounce of her being.

"You do real well against women, don't you?" Braden taunted.

Morgan had always had a temper—he felt ready to explode now—but his voice was even and cold when he spoke. "You'd better tell your sister to behave herself if she wants you to live beyond this day." His arms tightened around her. She wriggled to escape his hold, and he felt his body's reaction to it. It puzzled him. It infuriated him. He didn't like what he didn't understand, and he couldn't understand his reaction to this she-cat. She was trouble, pure trouble, but a part of him admired her, and he despised that admiration as a weakness in himself. "Tell her!"

"Lori."

Braden's voice was low but authoritative, and Morgan felt the girl relax slightly, then jerk away from him and run to her brother. Braden's handcuffed hands went over her head and around her, and he held her as she leaned trustingly against him. A criminal. A killer. A rare wave of loneliness swept over Morgan, flooding him with intense jealousy, nearly turning him inside out.

"Touching scene," he observed sarcastically, his voice rough as he tried to reestablish control—over his prisoner and the woman and over himself.

He tried to discipline his own body, to dismiss the

lingering flowery scent of Lorilee Braden, the re-membered softness of her body against his. She was a hellion, he warned himself, not soft at all, except in body. He'd already underestimated her twice. He wouldn't do it again.

# SCANDAL IN SILVER

## BY

## SANDRA CHASTAIN

"This delightful author has a tremendous talent that places her on a pinnacle reserved for special romance writers."—*Affaire de Coeur*

*Sandra Chastain is a true reader favorite, and with SCANDAL IN SILVER, her new "Once Upon a Time Romance," she borrows from Seven Brides for Seven Brothers for a wonderfully funny and sensual historical romance about five sisters stranded in the Colorado wilderness with a silver mine.*

"What was that?" he said, and came to a full stop.

To her credit she didn't jump up or cry out. Instead she looked around slowly, tilting her head to listen to the sounds of the night.

"I don't hear anything, Colter."

"We're being watched. Stand up slowly. Hold out your hand and smile."

She followed his directions, but the smiling was hard. She was certain there was nothing out there and that he knew it. This was a ruse. She'd known not to trust him; this proved it. "Now what?"

He returned her smile, dropped his wood and started toward her, speaking under his breath. "When I take your hand I'm going to put my arms around you and we'll walk deeper into the trees."

"Why?"

"I don't know what's going to happen, and I don't want to be out in the open." He hoped she didn't stop to examine that bit of inane logic.

"Shall I bring the rifle?"

"No, that would give us away."

He clasped her hand and pulled her close, sliding his arm around her as he turned her away from the fire. After an awkward moment she fitted herself against him and matched her steps to his.

"Is this good?" she asked, throwing her head back and widening her smile recklessly. The motion allowed her hat to fall behind her, freeing her hair and exposing her face to the light. She was rewarded by the astonished expression on his face. Two could play games, she decided.

His smile vanished. "Yes!" he said hoarsely. "You're getting the idea. In fact—"

"Don't you dare say I'm beautiful again, Captain Colter. Even a fool would know you are only trying to frighten me." She was looking up at him, her eyes stormy, her mouth soft and inviting. "Why?"

"I'm not trying to frighten you," he answered. She couldn't know how appealing she was, or that she was tempting him to kiss her. And he couldn't resist the temptation. He curled his arm, bringing her around in front of him as he lowered his head. His lips touched hers. She froze.

"Easy," he whispered, brushing his lips back and forth against a mouth now clamped shut. She gasped, parting her lips, and he thrust his tongue inside. Her jacket fell open as he pressed against her, almost dizzy from the feel of her. He felt her arm creep around him. For a long, senseless moment he forgot what he'd started out to do. The kiss that was meant to distract Sabrina had an unexpected effect on him.

Then she pulled back, returning them to reality. Her shock was followed by fear and finally anger. She slapped him, hard, with the palm of her healing hand.

Her eyes were wide. "What was all that about?" she asked as she backed away, one hand protectively across her chest, the other behind her.

"I don't know," he admitted ruefully, "but whatever it was, it's gone."

"I see. Then I don't suppose you'll need this now, will you?" She reached down and pulled the knife from her boot.

"No. I guess I won't."

"Concealing the knife in your bedroll was what this was about, wasn't it? Don't ever try something like that again, Captain Colter, or I'll use the knife on you."

She whirled around, and moments later she was inside the blanket, eyes closed, her entire body trembling like a snow rabbit caught in the gaze of a mountain lion.

She'd known there was nothing out there, but she'd let him play out his plan, wondering how far he'd go. She hadn't expected him to kiss her. But more than that she hadn't expected the blaze of fire that the kiss had ignited, the way her body had reached out, begging to be touched, the way her lips parted, inviting him inside.

"Guess you're not going to take the first watch," he finally said.

"You guessed right, soldier." Her throat was so tight that her words came out in a breathless rush.

"Got to you, did I?" he teased, surprising himself with the lightness of his tone. "The truth is, you got to me, too. But both of us know that nothing can come of it. No two people could ever be more un-suited to each other. It won't happen again."

"You're right, Colter. It won't. As for why I responded, perhaps I have my own ways of distraction."

Her claim was brave, but he didn't believe she'd kissed him intentionally. He didn't even try to analyze the kiss. Giving thought to the combustion only fueled the flame. Best to put it behind them.

"Sweet dreams, madam jailer. I hope you don't have nightmares. I'm unarmed."

Sabrina didn't answer. He was wrong. He had a weapon, a new and powerful one against which she had no defense. He'd started a wildfire and Sabrina felt as if she were burning up.

# THE WINDFLOWER

BY

# SHARON AND TOM CURTIS

"Sharon and Tom's talent is immense."
—LaVyrle Spencer

*With stories rich in passion and filled with humor, bestselling authors Sharon and Tom Curtis have become two of the most beloved romance novelists. Now this extraordinarily talented writing team offers a captivating tale of love and danger on the high seas, as a young woman is kidnapped and taken to an infamous privateering ship and her mysterious, golden-haired captor.*

"You're very amusing, you know," he said.

For the first time since she'd left the tavern, she felt an emotion stirring within her that was not terror.

"I wasn't aware that I was being amusing," she said, a terse edge to her voice.

"I never supposed you were aware of it. But don't you think you were being a little overly conscientious? Under the circumstances."

Unfortunately his statement hit uncomfortably close to the truth. Before she could stop herself, Merry bit out, "I suppose *you* think nothing of knocking whole villages to the ground."

"Nothing at all," he said cheerfully.

"And terrorizing innocent women!" she said, a tremble in her voice.

"Yes. Innocent ones," he said, running his palm along her flat stomach, "and not so innocent ones."

She nearly fainted under his touch. "Don't do that," she said, her voice cracking in good earnest.

"Very well," he said, removing his hand. He went back to lean against the porch, resting on the heels of his hands, his long finely muscled legs stretched before him, and gave her an easy smile. "Don't run away from me, little one. For the moment you're much safer here."

Something in her face made him laugh again. "I can see you don't believe it," he continued. "But stay with me nevertheless. If you run off, I'll have to chase you, and I don't think we want to scamper across the beach like a pair of puppies."

She wondered if that meant he wouldn't invest much energy in trying to catch her if she did try to run and if it might not be worth the risk.

Reading her thoughts with alarming precision, he asked good-humoredly, "Do you think you could outrun me?"

It was hardly likely. A man used to safely negotiating the rigging during a high wind would be quick enough to catch her before she could even think of moving, and strong enough to make her very sorry. Involuntarily her gaze dropped to his hard legs, with their smooth, rhythmical blend of healthy muscle.

"Like what you see?" he asked her.

Merry's gaze flew to his, and she blushed and swallowed painfully. In a ludicrously apologetic voice she managed, "I beg your pardon."

"That's quite all right." He reached out his hand and stroked beneath her chin. "Much too conscientious. Would it surprise you to know, my little friend, that having you stare at my legs is the most uplifting thing that's happened to me all day?"

It was not the kind of remark she had remotely conceived a man might make to a woman, but there was something in his matter-of-fact delivery that made her suspect that he had participated in a great many conversations in precisely this style. Wishing she could match the ease of his tone, she said, "It's a pity your days are so dull."

"Oh, yes," he said with a glimmer of amusement, "in between knocking down villages and making people walk the plank, pirates really have very little to do."

Merry wondered briefly how she could ever have been so foolish as to have actually *wished* for an adventure.

"I don't know how you can talk about it like that," she said weakly.

He smiled. "I take it you don't usually flirt with villains."

"I don't flirt with *anyone*," Merry said, getting angry.

"I believe you don't, darling."

For a second his kind, enticing gaze studied her face, and then he looked away to the south, where a tiny flicker began to weave through the rocks. Another star of light appeared, and another, dragon's breath in the night.

"My cohorts," he observed. Offering her a hand, Devon inclined his head toward the dark-blue shadows that crept along the tavern's north side. "Come with me, I'm sure you don't want them to see you."

"*More* pirates?" said Merry hoarsely, watching the lights.

"Six more. Seven, if Reade is sober."

She hesitated, not daring to trust him, her face turned to him with the unconscious appeal of a lost child.

"Come with me," he repeated patiently. "Look at it this way. Better one dreadful pirate than seven. Whatever you're afraid I'll do to you, I can only do it once. *They* can do it seven times. Besides, I'm unarmed. You can frisk me if you want." His arm came around her back, drawing her away from the tavern. Grinning down at her, he said, "As a matter of fact, I wish you would frisk me."

She went with him, her footsteps as passive as a dreamer.

It seemed quite unnecessary to tell him. Nevertheless Merry said, "I've never met anyone like you in my life."

And don't miss these thrilling
romances from Bantam Books,
on sale in November:

## *ADAM'S FALL*
by the *New York Times* bestselling author
### Sandra Brown

Now available in paperback!

## *PURE SIN*
by the mistress of erotic historical romance
### Susan Johnson

"Susan Johnson is one of the best."
—*Romantic Times*

## *ON WINGS OF MAGIC*
by the nationally bestselling
### Kay Hooper

"[Kay Hooper] writes with exceptional beauty and
grace."
—*Romantic Times*

# OFFICIAL RULES

To enter the sweepstakes below carefully follow all instructions found elsewhere in this offer.

The **Winners Classic** will award prizes with the following approximate maximum values: 1 Grand Prize: $26,500 (or $25,000 cash alternate); 1 First Prize: $3,000; 5 Second Prizes: $400 each; 35 Third Prizes: $100 each; 1,000 Fourth Prizes: $7.50 each. Total maximum retail value of Winners Classic Sweepstakes is $42,500. Some presentations of this sweepstakes may contain individual entry numbers corresponding to one or more of the aforementioned prize levels. To determine the Winners, individual entry numbers will first be compared with the winning numbers preselected by computer. For winning numbers not returned, prizes will be awarded in random drawings from among all eligible entries received. Prize choices may be offered at various levels. If a winner chooses an automobile prize, all license and registration fees, taxes, destination charges and, other expenses not offered herein are the responsibility of the winner. If a winner chooses a trip, travel must be complete within one year from the time the prize is awarded. Minors must be accompanied by an adult. Travel companion(s) must also sign release of liability. Trips are subject to space and departure availability. Certain black-out dates may apply.

The following applies to the sweepstakes named above:

**No purchase necessary.** You can also enter the sweepstakes by sending your name and address to: P.O. Box 508, Gibbstown, N.J. 08027. Mail each entry separately. Sweepstakes begins 6/1/93. Entries must be received by 12/30/94. Not responsible for lost, late, damaged, misdirected, illegible or postage due mail. Mechanically reproduced entries are not eligible. All entries become property of the sponsor and will not be returned.

**Prize Selection/Validations:** Selection of winners will be conducted no later than 5:00 PM on January 28, 1995, by an independent judging organization whose decisions are final. Random drawings will be held at 1211 Avenue of the Americas, New York, N.Y. 10036. Entrants need not be present to win. Odds of winning are determined by total number of entries received. Circulation of this sweepstakes is estimated not to exceed 200 million. All prizes are guaranteed to be awarded and delivered to winners. Winners will be notified by mail and may be required to complete an affidavit of eligibility and release of liability which must be returned within 14 days of date on notification or alternate winners will be selected in a random drawing. Any prize notification letter or any prize returned to a participating sponsor, Bantam Doubleday Dell Publishing Group, Inc., its participating divisions or subsidiaries, or the independent judging organization as undeliverable will be awarded to an alternate winner. Prizes are not transferable. No substitution for prizes except as offered or as may be necessary due to unavailability, in which case a prize of equal or greater value will be awarded. Prizes will be awarded approximately 90 days after the drawing. All taxes are the sole responsibility of the winners. Entry constitutes permission (except where prohibited by law) to use winners' names, hometowns, and likenesses for publicity purposes without further or other compensation. Prizes won by minors will be awarded in the name of parent or legal guardian.

**Participation:** Sweepstakes open to residents of the United States and Canada, except for the province of Quebec. Sweepstakes sponsored by Bantam Doubleday Dell Publishing Group, Inc., (BDD), 1540 Broadway, New York, NY 10036. Versions of this sweepstakes with different graphics and prize choices will be offered in conjunction with various solicitations or promotions by different subsidiaries and divisions of BDD. Where applicable, winners will have their choice of any prize offered at level won. Employees of BDD, its divisions, subsidiaries, advertising agencies, independent judging organization, and their immediate family members are not eligible.

Canadian residents, in order to win, must first correctly answer a time limited arithmetical skill testing question. Void in Puerto Rico, Quebec and wherever prohibited or restricted by law. Subject to all federal, state, local and provincial laws and regulations. For a list of major prize winners (available after 1/29/95): send a self-addressed, stamped envelope entirely separate from your entry to: Sweepstakes Winners, P.O. Box 517, Gibbstown, NJ 08027. Requests must be received by 12/30/94. DO NOT SEND ANY OTHER CORRESPONDENCE TO THIS P.O. BOX.

SWP 7/93